The University of Sydney Anthology 2012

DARLINGTON PRESS

First published 2012 by Darlington Press

Darlington Press is an imprint of SYDNEY UNIVERSITY PRESS

Funded by The University of Sydney Union and The University of Sydney Faculty of Arts and Social Sciences

Images and some short quotations have been used in this book. Every effort has been made to identify and attribute credit appropriately. The editors thank contributors for permission to reproduce their work.

Reproduction and Communication for other purposes

Fisher Library F03

University of Sydney

NSW 2006 Australia

Email: sup.info@sydney.edu.au

National Library of Australia Cataloguing-in-Publication entry

Title: Sparks : the University of Sydney anthology 2012 /
           [University of Sydney students] ; foreword by Mark Tredinnick.
ISBN: 9781921364273 (pbk.)
Subjects: College students' writings, Australian--New South Wales--Sydney.
           Short stories, Australian--21st century.
Other Authors/Contributors:
           University of Sydney.
Dewey Number:
           A820.8004

Cover design by the 2012 Anthology Editorial Committee

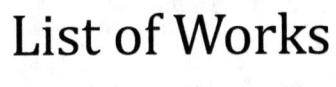

List of Works

FICTION

NON-FICTION

POETRY

PHOTOGRAPHY

Foreword

Getting Over Your Self

Mark Tredinnick

I hardly meet a person who doesn't think they have a book in them – who doesn't want, or think they ought to want, to write their life story, or someone's life story, a novel, a poem or two, a film script.

The desire to write is close to universal.

And so I said on radio on the morning of the day in Newcastle, when I sat at last to write this foreword. ABC Radio Newcastle had asked me on to talk about a writing workshop I had come to town to run and about a reading I was giving later. The interviewer and I talked on air a little about the numbers for the workshop, which were very strong. Which had kept growing and growing until the organisers had to call a halt.

Sometimes I think there can be no-one left out there who never felt the urge, the itch at least, to write, and I said so. Jill was surprised. We writers and journalists like to think that we're alone – the poet in the garret, the novelist in his shed, the memoirist writing by torchlight at the window down the hall, the children finally asleep. Alone at our work, maybe, but not in our ambition.

'You really think so,' she probed.

'I do.'

'Why do you think it is so many people want to write, then?'

And so it was I found myself wondering out loud, exploring my accidental thesis, about the universality of the writing urge (if not the writing gene, of which more soon). Maybe, I suggested, it's an aspect of the hopeless hope each of us harbours – knowing, without ever quite accepting, that our time here will end – to outlive our lives; to make a mark that outstays us; to leave a trace, in particular, of our own voice, that ephemeral vessel that seems to float our very self into the world. A written work, one sometimes imagines, might leave *me* behind – a boat that still floats me, when I, myself, am sunk. If I wrote a story people remembered, if I wrote a bit of a book about that plane that crashed in the ranges in the eighties, if I put down some tales about my mother's life or the trauma of my arrival by sinking boat out of trouble, if I turned a poem people recited to their lover or quoted at funerals, if I wrote a script that became a film, my voice would go on speaking, and speaking me, a long time after I myself am gone.

She looked skeptical.

Perhaps I was giving too much of myself away, too early in the morning.

I pulled on the reins. The urge to write isn't all about posterity. Some people write for fame or, God help them, for fortune. Some people write to get laid. There are faster paths, cheaper, but still. In nobler moments I've been known to say that each of us, particularly those of us as fortunate as I am, have been given the world – life, the weather, the birds, art, children, love, language, the works – and writing is a way of giving it back, of returning the gift, of acknowledging it all. Not in order to live forever. Just to reciprocate. To say thanks. There are many things I can't do, or don't, many other ways I might return the gift, but don't or don't know how to; writing is a thing I love, a thing I've studied and practised (I would never say mastered). It is a way I know to live deliberately, as Thoreau put it – mindfully. A way to live large and go deep and not leave a hell of a mess behind. So I write. And there are other writers who share, I'm sure, this sense of writing as an offering, an offering back, a vote of thanks. Writing, for some, isn't about immortality or celebrity; it's what used to be known as a calling: an activity to which one feels not just compelled but commanded.

'And there's more,' I said. Warming to this. Writing for me is a way of making sense: of me, of the world, of the absurd miracle of being on earth and trying to live well and do some good and know some peace and make some love in the few years each of us gets to live this dream rounded by sleep. Writing is a kind of divination, a madness that makes, as Emily Dickinson said, the divinest sense. Of the mysterious world of matter and mind and memory that surrounds us. Writing, wrote Wallace Stevens, another poet, is a 'rage for order', by way of language; a search of pattern, a patterning, amid the chaos. Writing, all art, is a stay against despair – though making it is the most maddening thing I know. Still, the days I write in are the days I most deeply and thoroughly, honestly live. Not orderly, not by any means, but shapely, chosen, real. One never orders the world, but sometimes one orders one's head for a while; sometimes one makes a poem. A story. And it's an unaccountably consoling, yogic, business – more than an experience; a long drawn out, arduous epiphany.

Poetry, writes Jane Hirshfield, makes through language what meditation makes through silence. Makes *in* language what yoga makes *in* silence. Although it's often, especially in prose, a process much less like prayer and much more like battle. Sometimes it's like a party. Sometimes a good one. A rave.

'Writing, for me, is like love,' I went on: hard to find, harder to make, harder still to keep, but addictive and beautiful, and capable of asking better questions of myself and insisting on more honest answers than anything else I do or know. Writing for me, though it draws on and trades in all things, 'is apart from all things,' as Jack Gilbert puts it. Like love.

'Okay,' she said. I'd ended up a long way from where we started.

'So, what tips would you give someone who wanted to get some writing done?'

What I wanted to say – but didn't, since I had a course to pitch – was that, though everyone wants to write, most people probably shouldn't. The gift for writing – not to mention the graft and the mad dedication entailed in learning and practising the craft of it – is not nearly so widely distributed as the desire to make it. Again, like love … Writing's much harder than it looks. It hurts; it pays poorly; it takes time; it loses you friends; it's bad for your posture. Unless you're sure you'd feel you hadn't lived the one life you were meant to, says Rilke to the young poet, if you didn't get to write, if they didn't put 'poet' on your gravestone – don't write. It's hard work, and most of the hard work isn't the syntax or the personal discipline – though those are hard enough. Most of it is the spiritual hard yards you have to keep putting in, long after the athletes have retired and stopped rising at dawn to run the track or swim the pool – the heavy lifting involved in getting out of your own way for long enough to hear whatever it is that wants to speak itself to and through you, and to get that down on page.

I'm sure I heard the great novelist Jonathan Franzen say the other day (he was on radio this time) that what writing's for is 'becoming', and I think he meant something like what I mean here: the larger part of the practice of writing is an endless getting over yourself, a peeling off of masks; it's a stepping out of the disguises in which one lives, in which one has, to some extent, to lead one's daily lives. Writing entails working your way back to who you really are and how you really speak about whatever it is that counts for you in your very own original voice.

Which takes me back to the tip I offered on air.

No two of us are identical; none of us is a clone. The Greeks thought that each of us played host to a genius, a one-off intelligence, a singular way of seeing and being. A self. And that's always seemed about right to me. It is, I think, one's self, in its essential self, that each of us who aspires to write wants to voice and leave behind. The book you want to write, I think, is the book that only you *can* write – the one told in the voice that tells *you* (the unique ecosystem that is the life of your mind and memory, this unique intelligence, this unprecedented self) in every phrase, no matter what or whom it's *about*. No matter what its subject, no matter if it's memoir, essay, new journalism, lyric or heroic poem, or fiction. And it turns out that such a book, such a story – unique in its *telling*, if not in its tale – such a poem, touches a reader like no other kind of writing, maybe like no other kind of art – almost as though it was that reader's very own book, written not only *for* her, but *by* her. Its singular voice becomes, by the alchemy of story, by an integrity of telling, the reader's own singular voice; its self, her self.

Each original story is a proof of integrity, a proof against anonymity; each poem is a flame that refused to go out, a silence that would not be kept. That could almost be our own. Beyond good storylines and great sex and shock-horror and smart moves and wisecrackery and assorted cleverness, this is why we read: to know that we are not alone in our solitude. To know that each solitude counts. That each solitude counts uniquely. In particular, one's own.

How I write, said Joan Didion somewhere, is who I am. Or it is who I think I am, or am pretending to be, or trying not to be. And the point is that one's speaking voice, one's way of talking on paper, gives one's self away. And the stories and poems that reach us and last are those that ring true, those that go closest to escaping pretence. That say *I am*, and *you are, too*, in every phrase.

And if all this is even halfway true, we could all take Hemingway's advice. And this was my tip. Never write anything that goes the way you've heard it put before. If it's been said, it's been said: those are no longer your words to utter, and if you utter them, they'll have nothing new to say, and nothing to say, in particular, about you. Your writing will be second-hand; your voice will not be in it; your poem will stay stuck on the page; your story will roll over and go back to sleep, taking your reader with it. Resist all cliché: that was Hemingway's tip, and it was the one I thought to say on air. Write everything fresh. Make every phrase new.

Jill seemed to think that might be worth trying.

'You want another one?' I asked.

'Sure.'

Never write to please anyone else. Write to please yourself, as William Faulkner put it (another dead white American male, admittedly) – but make yourself very hard to please. The question is not who's listening; what counts, as Francine Prose puts it, is who's talking. Are you writing like yourself, or as someone like yourself; as someone more likeable, perhaps? Cooler? More bankable?

In his essay 'Pain Won't Kill You' – a commencement address he made at Kenyon College in May 2011 – Jonathan Franzen had some hard words to say about the manufactured selves we parade in the fast and narcissistic commerce of Facebook, the 'liking' that realm trades in, and the superficial, self-serving banter one uses there to engender that 'liking' and to write the movie, in which one stars. 'I may be overstating the case, a little bit,' he concedes. 'Very probably,' he goes on, 'you're sick to death of hearing social media dissed by cranky 51-year-olds.' (Subtract a year, and this might be me talking.) But he doesn't come to trash, he says; he comes to speak a word for literature and love. 'My aim here,' he says, 'is mainly to set up a contrast between the narcissistic tendencies of technology and the problem of actual love.'

To love someone or something is to be thrown back against who you really are; it is to get over the addiction to being liked; it is to find out that you are not, or not always, the likeable, cool dude you would like the world to think you are. To love is to dedicate yourself to someone or something not, in truth, capable of being liked all the time. To love, in the actual world, is to become real; it is to engage with the real, paradoxical, multiple, contradictory world. And so it is with writing – which for Franzen, as for me, is like love in what it costs and what it yields; in its practice and its texture. 'If you're moved to return the gift that other people's fiction represents for you,' Franzen goes on, alluding to another reason many people write (joining the conversation other books start us on), 'you eventually can't ignore what's fraudulent or secondhand in your pages.'

To write, as to love, is not to consume the world from a safe distance, or to package yourself and sell it to the world. It is not to *like* the world or to ask it to *like* you back. To write is to become who you really are, by stages; it is to let the world be what the world is. To write is an act of love, and like love it hurts, and like love it heals. It's not *about* you, but it does remake you; and in every word you speak – the poem you make, the story you tell, the landscape you lovingly draw – you speak who you are, or who you are becoming.

How does writing hurt, and how does it hurt like love? There's the risk of rejection. There's rejection, itself. There are all the ways you suddenly discover you know how *not* to say what you see and how you feel and to sound like who you are; all the ways you try, and inevitably fail, to please. All the ways the position you find yourself in – this place, this plot, this paragraph – doesn't fit the story you had told yourself you were.

Writing is love, then, and like love it hurts. But, as Franzen concludes: 'pain hurts, but it doesn't kill. When you consider the alternative – an anaesthetised dream of self-sufficiency, abetted by technology – pain emerges as the natural product and natural indicator of being alive in the world.' Love is the real life Facebook keeps at bay; literature writes the real world the Twittersphere keeps behind glass.

Writing, for the writer, is a way of coming true. It's a way of 'being alive in the world'. And I think I'd add: of coming alive *to* the world.

Writing can become a means of leading what Jane Hirshfield calls a thoroughly lived life – the kind of life, in fact, any writer is going to need to lead if they're going to write a poem or a story worth reading – a work that rings true.

Which is a way of edging up on what literature does for readers, too – what writing, beyond saving the life of the writer, does for the rest of us. There are many answers to that question, but they come down, I reckon, to these two.

1. Literature saves language from ourselves. It steals language back from the market and returns it in its fullness to us.

Good stories and poems redeem language from the chatter of everyday discourse, from the banalities of the marketplace and the parliament, the ethernet and the small screen; from the clichés and sentimentality we trade in at home and on the sidelines and in the boardroom, and on commercial radio; from the moral absolutism of discourse of church and state and corner store; from the grand and obtuse abstractions of theory, policy and the various professions. Which is to say literature gives language back to itself. And to us. It resists.

It uses language with rigour and affection; it makes language new; it remembers its rhythms and the vernacular music it makes in our mouths. Literature remembers, and lets us remember, that language is a speech act, an enactment profoundly human. It puts words back in their bodies. And in our bodies. Literature recharges language. It conserves it. It reminds us how good the right words in the right order can be, and how much bigger and realer they can make the world seem.

A little while ago, Judith Beveridge, who knows my affection for the writing of the American poet Charles Wright, and who shares it, sent me these words of his, which speak, the way that literature speaks, for what it is that literature does for language and, therefore, for us all:

> without poetry there's just talk. Talk is cheap and proves nothing. Poetry is dear and difficult to come by. But it poles us across the river and puts a music in our ears. It moves us to contemplation. And what we contemplate, what we sing our hymns to and offer our prayers to, is what will reincarnate us in the natural world, and what will be our one hope for salvation in the What'sToCome.

2. And the second thing literature does – telling its stories, making its poems, singing its songs, bearing its witness?

Literature gives *us* back to ourselves. It gives us back to our lives.

Literature writes lives and places in their everyday complexity, their contradiction and their beautiful – not always likeable, but truthful and therefore lovable – actuality. Literature, says Alice Munro, writes 'the things within things'. Literature writes the texture of existence; it tells the inner life of actual life – of moments, of dramas, of places, of episodes, of lives and deaths. Depicting life as it runs beyond the reach of marketing categories and demographic segments, literature unsettles settled morality and conventional wisdom; it pricks pomposity; it unseats cliché; it disassembles fundamentalisms; it reminds us who we really are when we're not pretending; it forgives us for being human. As Mark Strand says of poetry, literature 'allows us to have the life we are denied because we are too busy living' inside the tropes of family, society, fashion, commerce and convention. In other words, it gives us back the fullness of our lives. It makes us think twice. It reminds us that what one sees is far less than all there is to get; that how things look is rarely what they are; that how we position ourselves is rarely who – and never all – we are.

And something like all this – this looking into the inner life of actuality, this resuscitation of language, this becoming through syntax, this bringing of the world to life, this resistance, this falling into stories as if into love – you'll find attempted – sometimes with astonishing craft, everywhere earnestly – in the pieces in this anthology, a selection of the work of students at the University of Sydney in 2012. It would be asking too much of these young works to have them bear the weight of my aspirations for literature into this slick, often glib and ever more narcissistic digital world; it would be wrong to expect them all to do everything Charles Wright hopes for from a poem, to practise the kind of love Jonathan Franzen looks for in story, to pull off the deep integrity Joan Didion listens for in memoir, to observe the ferocious originality Hemingway demanded of every phrase of everything. I'm pretty sure some of these writers have other ambitions in mind, and so they should. But there's very good work here in all manner of different voices and forms, from erotica via noir and new journalism to sci-fi and North

Coast Raymond Carver – shorts and riffs and imaginings and plaints, an unruly choir of attitude, affection, addiction and affliction. There are three or four brilliant pieces (I'll let you decide which I mean), and many memorable passages, enough to give one hope that literature, which has such urgent, slow work to do for language and for all of us in the years ahead, has fallen into some good new hands.

Congratulations to everyone who made the cut, and to the editors for pulling together such a lively, edgy ensemble.

I should probably tell you something about the stand-out pieces here, but I'd rather let you find your own way through. That's what literature asks us to do, readers and writers.

Instead, let these samples, like stray birds, fly some of the wood to you from the trees; let them suggest the vivacity, the verve and spunk, not to mention the caroling multiplicity, of thought and voice this anthology is alive with.

If he fled the scene of a crime, he would be described as brown haired, of medium build. Surely he has some reserve of luck that he's never had to touch before. Are you saying you want to have sex with my wife? 'An abandoned future,' Clotho said. She rarely called her friends in China; there was nothing to tell them. In the blue scent of forgotten boughs. It was just as pretty a story as you were. You wondered what answers he was looking for. I must inform you that it's me you love, not him. What beauty it dons and its body so bronze. I'm as predictable as their minimum wages. Suddenly there's a mushroom and then another. Past scenes stitched like patchwork scraps onto the present. Study me with your brittle smile. Miras saw a flock of birds, doves perhaps, scatter as a loud BANG reverberated. Phone held tight to his ear jabbering away but always looking around … like he was looking for someone looking for him. As sunlight through our green ceiling fades. He tugged an absent smile across is lips. The town hall was reborn to us that evening. Pissing's become a gauntlet. He was young and dumb and out to impress. You'll eat well at my place, Fabullus, if you're lucky, and you bring plenty of pizza and a hot babe and some goon and a good mood. 'Vegetarian nearly killed by a little chicken.' I'll meet you where your spine ends. This isn't really how it happened. When she closed her eyes I felt as if I was alone in the room. Illicit footprints, the words of the dead. I got on a bus, taking it all the way to Oxford Street, where I got off outside an underwear shop.

Sparks

Do You Believe in Rock and Roll?

Agnes Bairstow

Hank is an RSL singer. He has an open face and darting eyes that people would probably describe as 'twinkling' if they were blue. His eyes are brown, so they do not. Hank's face is a bland one, and if he fled from the scene of a crime he would be described as brown haired, of medium build. Hank has never wished to be striking. He's not an entertainer, just a singer. He doesn't sing his own songs, only other people's. He occasionally scribbles lyrics onto the back of envelopes, but can never seem to link them together. Hank drives himself all around the state and does three or four performances a week. He places no artistic expectations on himself, only hopes for money and songs and steak, and maybe at some indeterminate time in the future a different expectation.

Hank's father had a faded greyish tattoo of Ned Kelly on his right shoulder. He liked country music and alliteration. He was a sporadically self-educated labourer and the life of the local pub and Hank likes to tell himself that although his father died young, he died content. Hank remembers very little of his mother: a swishing nylon dress, her vinyl beauty case on the laminex table. She moved to the city when Hank was yet too small to realise he would miss her. 'She wanted more,' Hank's father would say. 'I hope she found it.'

Hank's father loved his record player. Childhood reverberated with the hisses and pops of Nanna's old 78s and Dad's vinyl LPs, brittle brown paper sandwiched between their black glossy surfaces. The smell of them, dark and rich, Hank's church incense, his mother's perfume. Hank's father would take out a record and set it on the platter reverently, and all through Hank's childhood they ate their bachelor's meals in silent appreciation of Johnny Cash and Hank Williams and Patsy Cline. They played cards to Slim Dusty and late at night, maybe at Christmas, Hank's father would get a little bit drunk and maudlin and put on a classical music sampler with a picture of an orchestra pit on the front.

Hank brought home his first guitar at fifteen and sat down with it on the pastel vinyl couch in the lounge room. His father said very little, just sat there and watched him play.

'Go on mate, play something else.'

A week or so before Hank arrives in town, a black and white laser-printed sheet with a murky picture of him standing behind a microphone is pinned up to a noticeboard or a coming attractions board. Hank has a Gibson Les Paul and a drum machine and a microphone. He sets himself up in the corner of the front bar or up on the stage. He plays 'Hotel California' and 'Magic Carpet Ride' for the dope soaked bearded seventies burnouts who hang around the bar in coastal towns. He plays Hank Williams and Johnny Cash for the older folks. He plays Bon Jovi and Cold Chisel for the slightly younger folks and Powderfinger for kids who look like they'd rather be anywhere else than a town with two pokie machines and a bowling club with a sparse lawn.

Hank had a sign-writer friend make him a sign. He used to have a handwritten one, but he finds the neatness of the new sign soothing. He hangs the sign on the front of the drum machine: *'YES!' I TAKE REQUESTS.*

In the first year that he was touring, a neatly dressed man with neatly side-parted Brylcreemed hair sidled up to the mic stand as Hank took a sip from his water bottle. He asked for 'Crying' by Roy Orbison. Hank flipped through the sixties folder and found the song. When he played it a couple of the older couples leaned closer to each other and held hands. But the old man just sat there. Hank remembers that very well.

What Hank likes the most is the unembarrassed couples who get up to dance when he does songs like 'American Pie' and 'Eagle Rock' and 'December 1963 (Oh What A Night)'. Sometimes they have radiant smiles and clumsy dance steps and Hank thinks yes, this is it. He thinks of his father sitting at the kitchen chair, saying 'Go on mate, play something else.' Leaning forward, his hands clasped between his knees, rollie between two knuckles.

The RSL in this town is big. It has a restaurant that sells passable Australian-Chinese and excellent steaks. Hank loves RSL steaks. Porterhouse monsters and limp salads drowned in gravy. Hank loves the beer-sweat smell when he performs and he wonders how many late nights he's spent eating a complimentary steak as the kitchen staff close up and hose everything down. A steak and a beer and the polyester hotel room seems less claustrophobic. He can go to sleep to the late movie, a pay-per-view movie if the hotel is any good.

There is a huge bank of pokie machines. Six o'clock on a Thursday night and Hank can hear the busy electronic sound of them as he walks across the lobby. Hank dislikes pokies, hates the pull of the blooping noises and the waxy look that faces get, bathed in the light of the screen. They give him an empty cold feeling sometimes, and he has to close that door in his mind, close it on the blank faces and the jingling coins.

Hank is due to start at eight. He sets up his equipment on a small raised wooden area at the back of the main bar. It's carpeted and has a sterile air-conditioning smell overlaid with beer. To one side there is a glass cabinet filled with tennis trophies and war medals.

The gig goes well. The crowd is a nice mix, well-dressed cockies in town for the night, some young kids, a couple of old club regulars who look like they turned up for the ham raffle ten years ago and have been sitting at the bar ever since.

There's a group of men at the bar. They're dressed in tight blue jeans and R. M. Williams boots and most of them have red outdoor faces. One of them comes over to the mic and passes a ten dollar note to Hank.

'You don't need to do that,' Hank says. 'Pick a song, I'll play it.'

The man smiles back with beery generosity. 'Keep it anyway,' he says. He leafs through Hank's books and chooses two songs. 'It's me mate's birthday,' he says. 'I fucken love that fella.' Hank has never had a male friend he loved enough to say that sort of thing, certainly not to a stranger. He likes the man for that, for his big rough hands and Cold Chisel t-shirt.

Hank plays 'Don't Dream It's Over' for the men, and they all stand at the bar and sing it. One of the barmen crosses his arms but the rest of them smile indulgently. And halfway through the chorus ('hey now hey now') Hank has a strange feeling. He feels as if he's done this before, as if he has sung this very song with the same canned drum machine beat for another group of drunken men. All of a sudden he can see a whole line of drunken crowds behind him, five years of them, all the nights he's stood in little towns like this and sung other people's songs. Hank doesn't know if he has any songs. Even if he did he sure as fuck doesn't sing them.

But the feeling goes away like it always does and he finishes the song and the drunk man from before throws his arm around a shorter guy and Hank can see, even from up on the little stage, that he loves him. Hank doesn't know how the people in this town come at that. He thinks of all the little towns he's been in, all the secrets and ugliness and he hopes it turns out okay. Maybe these men don't even think of it as love. Maybe it's mateship. Maybe deep down in their own silent realisation of their wants and needs they call it love. Hank hopes they do.

'Happy birthday, Steve,' Hank says into the microphone, and he smiles. Because that's what he does.

There'll be a wake tomorrow morning so Hank packs up his equipment and moves it out to his car straight after the gig. When he's taken the drum machine and the guitar he comes back for the mic stand. There's a woman sitting on the wooden edge of the stage, staring at her phone. She's wearing tight jeans and a looser shirt and leather boots. Her hair is blonde and wispy in a hairdresser kind of way. She works behind the bar. Hank doesn't know how he can tell this, but he can. It's a sixth sense. Hank has been mothered by women who work behind bars, and thrown out of bars by men who work behind bars. He knows bar people. Her face is young.

'Nice show,' she says.

'If you like that sort of thing,' Hank says.

'As a matter of fact I do.'

She's maybe fifteen years older than Hank and kind of quiet and well spoken. Nice is the word that comes to mind. But Hank is tired and he wants his beer and gravy-drowned steak, so he says 'I'll be performing tomorrow night as well,' and leaves.

Hank puts Triple J on as he's driving back to the hotel. A kid from Broken Hill rings up to request a song. Triple J was like samizdat when Hank was growing up. Now there's the internet. Hank feels like a relic.

This is a flat town out in the wheat belt. As Hank was driving into town the sun was setting, and all the barren stubbled fields were bathed in liquid gold. Now it's dark and cold and when he winds down the window all Hank can smell is dust and smoke. The motel backs onto the Coles. Hank wonders in that vague window-shopping way that he does more and more what it would be like to live here. Out on acres, away from the screaming voices that spill out of the four main street pubs at closing time. The sky hanging above, dark and full of stars. Quiet. But Hank never gets so far as to imagine growing anything. Just imagines the land empty and green around him. The ticking of a ute engine. The radio playing inside.

Halfway through the set. The crowd is different tonight, a bit younger, a bit rougher. He plays some newer stuff, some older stuff, some bland stuff. He's playing a song he's done so many times he could do it in a drunken coma. His eyes fix on the announcements behind the bar and he realises that not only is there a meat tray raffle tomorrow but that today is the day his father would have been sixty.

When he gets to the end of the song there is sporadic applause; the murmur of the crowd remains constant. Most of the time Hank is only one step above a jukebox. Sky TV is real entertainment. Hank's about as cheesy as the green and gold eighties carpet and the mock vintage beer ads up on the wall. He knows this, it's just unsettling to be reminded of it. In the lulls between songs he takes sips of water. He can hear plates knocking together in the kitchen, the ever-present blooping of the pokies.

Hank moves the capo from the head of his guitar to the second fret, then he plays 'Old Man'. It's quiet and unassuming, those first few riffs. Hank leans hard on the bended notes and he's singing it, but at the same time he's in the passenger seat of his dad's old bench seat Holden, smelling sun-warmed leather and oil, and he's content.

The woman is back again. She was working behind the bar tonight. Her eyes are puffy and tired but her skin is clear, even under the fluorescent lights.

'Want a beer?'

'Yes, please,' Hank says, and he follows her over to the bar.

'Tooheys Extra Dry,' he says, and he watches silently as she takes a cold schooner from beneath the bar, pours the beer, and waits for the head to settle. He's thirsty and his ears are ringing a little bit. When he reaches for his wallet she shakes her head and says 'Don't worry about it.'

Hank's steak and gravy hasn't arrived yet and he's already on his second beer, feeling jolly with it.

'So,' she says. 'Is your name really Hank?'

'Yes.' Hank takes a sip of beer and notices as he puts the glass to his lips that they're slightly numb. Hank has drunk in pubs and clubs from Queensland down through to the outskirts of Sydney and he's still a lightweight. Drank four beers and spewed onto the floor of his best friend's car at sixteen, all downhill from there.

'You playing again tomorrow night?'

'Nah,' Hank says. 'I'm moving on.'

Hank finds himself explaining through his slightly uncooperative lips the origin of the term 'jerkwater'. When the railroad across America was first founded, there were a lot of little one-horse towns where fresh water would have to be 'jerked' onto the steam trains bucket by bucket.

'Jerkwater towns,' he says. 'I like that.'

The waitress pauses slightly as she wipes down the bar, and Hank realises with an almost palpable stab of regret that he can't remember her name.

'You think this is a jerkwater town?'

'Nah,' he says. 'You've got a Coles.'

There's a half-eaten steak in front of him, and he must have begun it although he doesn't remember. Things are going fast and slow, suffused with incredible detail one minute, blurry the next. He's got 'Old Man' stuck in his head. Twenty-four and there's so much more.

'Why do you do all this old folk's music, Hank?'

'It's not … It's not work.'

She pours a beer for another customer. The chinking noise of change in the tip glass. She sets a beer down in front of Hank. He didn't even need to ask. He didn't want to.

'What's your favourite song?'

Hank loves being asked this question.

'I did it tonight. "Old Man".'

She laughs. 'You're an old man, son.'

Hank gets up and goes to the toilet, and when he gets back to the bar he knows that he's going to go out to his car. He puts a fifty dollar note in the tip jar. He wants to say something to the woman but she's at the other end of the bar and he doesn't know her name, so he puts his jacket on and goes outside, through the sliding doors and the nostril-shrinking fug of smoke coming from the beer garden. Then he's beside his car and he's talking to the woman. She has his keys in his hand.

You're going to stop me, Hank thinks. *You're going to stop me. We're going to go back inside and we'll keep talking and maybe later you'll take me back to your place and we'll make love.* That's what happens.

'You're too drunk to drive, son,' she says. 'I don't want to see any more crosses up on telegraph poles.'

Hank wonders what he's been saying to her. He wants to go inside with her, he really does, but he sees the bouncer walking across the car park and his dormant adolescent fight-or-fly instinct kicks in. All he knows is that he has to leave. He doesn't know why. He reaches out and snatches his keys out of her hand, even while in his mind they're walking back across the car park, he's going inside with her. Like he's seeing a future that doesn't exist.

He gets the car going okay. Then he's driving away. He doesn't know why he's doing it. He's afraid. He wishes he was back inside with the woman. They could talk some more about music. Hank gets drunk in bars a lot, abuses the hospitality of bowling clubs and pubs and barmen. He's never done this before, never driven. Surely he has some reserve of luck that he's never had to touch before.

'I never sing them,' Hank says to himself. Then a new rhythm comes into his head, a new song, and it's something good. He laughs as he hears it running through his head, laughs into the headlights that glance across his face from passing cars.

Footprints

Elizabeth J. Heller

Gavin parked his car on the street. He normally enjoyed walking down the long driveway to Mandy and Jack's house in the woods. Tonight he took his time, looking at the small snow-covered pine that he helped plant in March. He rubbed his neck; the muscle felt sore. He hadn't slept well last night because his thoughts were busy racing around the possibilities of why Jack and Mandy wanted to talk to him alone tonight. It could be nothing, but Mandy hadn't had a chance to let him know if it was something important.

Yesterday at the law office, Mandy and Gavin were both crowded at Gavin's desk staring at the case file on his computer screen. Mandy saw the time and rested her head on her hands, her elbows on his desk.

'Gavin, I've got to pack up. The nanny has to leave at six sharp tonight and Jack won't be home until after ten. You are coming for dinner tomorrow night, right?'

Her elbow was almost touching his. She was still looking at the screen. He pushed his chair back to give himself some space and watched her.

Mandy's short brown hair was pointed to the right from running her hand through it. As her blue eyes scanned the document, her fingers rolled the beads on her necklace. She moved her chair to face him and straightened her dress over her knees.

'I already told you I'm coming.'

Mandy liked to have dinner parties; she always said it was a good excuse to cook a more formal meal. Gavin had an open invitation and came most Saturday nights, though the other guests varied. Most were couples with kids and sometimes Mandy's family came.

'Who else is coming? Is your sister bringing a new friend?'

She started stuffing her laptop and papers into her bag. 'It's just you.'

'Just me? Did everyone else cancel?'

'No, Jack and I want to talk to you about something.' She was fastening her coat and didn't look up.

'About what?'

Mandy collapsed back into her chair. 'You know how much Jack and I enjoy your friendship,' she said. 'Just a minute,' she took her phone from her pocket, read the screen, and pushed herself up from the chair. 'Sorry, I've got to get home.'

'Is it important?' He glanced at his computer to check the time. She should make home by six o'clock. Her coat hung cockeyed. 'You missed a button,' he said.

'Oh, thanks.' She buttoned it, pulled on her hat and headed for the door. 'See you tomorrow at six o'clock then.' She walked out.

Gavin had replayed the scene dozens of times since yesterday, trying to finish Mandy's sentence. Was Mandy going to quit her job as a lawyer? They had shared an office since they were first-year associates, now five years ago. If so, why would she need Jack there to tell him? Before Mandy had kids, she and Gavin had spent more time together at the law firm than with their respective partners. His former fiancée Victoria was a paediatric resident and Mandy's husband Jack was an orthopaedic surgeon. Most days Gavin and Mandy had eaten lunch and dinner together. Now that she had kids, she only worked afternoons and always went home in time to eat dinner with the twins. They talked about cases, office politics, and in the early days had debated whether watching sports or wedding planning was a worse way to spend the free hours on the weekend. Mandy was the first person Gavin told when Victoria had left him six months before the wedding. He hadn't planned to tell anyone, but Mandy had noticed that the standard blue desktop had replaced the picture of Victoria on his computer. He had tried to pass it off as an accident, but his voice winced with the lie and before he knew it Mandy had closed the door to their office and asked if he wanted to be alone or tell her about it. Since then he had been a regular at her and Jack's Saturday night dinner parties. He guessed Mandy was trying to set him up some of the time, but he wasn't interested. He had put his emotions on ice. He hadn't seen much of Victoria once her residency started and they had decided not to live together before marriage. So it was easy to imagine that he didn't see Victoria because she was in the midst of an intense rotation at the hospital even though more than a year had passed since they had parted. He concentrated on work, and he figured that once he had made partner at the firm he would deal with his personal life.

The pine tree was almost as tall as Gavin now and someday it would intertwine with the other white branches forming a canopy over the driveway. The scenery he passed while walking up to the lit house reminded him of returning home from school for dinner as a kid. He veered off the shovelled path into the snow placing his large boot prints directly next to a pair of tiny ones. The light was on in the garage. He stood in the doorway almost expecting to see his father, but instead Jack was bent over the engine of the mustang.

'Hey Jack, need any help?'

Jack looked up. He was wearing a football jersey with 'coach' written across the front. His broad shoulders filled the space where the pads would go.

'No thanks, just checking the mechanic's work.'

'Anything unusual happen this week?'

'Are you telling me you didn't watch the game on Thursday, Gav? I think that was the highlight of my whole week …'

Jack was devoted to watching sports, and by now he must know Gavin didn't follow a single team or sport. Gavin tried to nod appropriately during Jack's monologue about the Thursday night game, but he wasn't really listening. Apparently, Jack saw nothing out of the ordinary about this night. Did he know that Gavin was the only guest and did he know what they were going to talk about? He thought maybe now was the time he should tell Jack that no-one called him Gav. He found it annoying. Instead, he waited until Jack had relived the goal or whatever had been scored on Thursday and said, 'If you don't need help, I think I'll go inside and see if Mandy could use a hand.'

Gavin continued up the stone path from the garage to the house. Something smelled good inside and he could make out Mandy and the kids in the kitchen through the French doors. Mandy was standing in front of the stove, her short brown hair dusted with flour. A pink-striped apron was tied with a big bow around her small waist. Hadley and Henry were tracking flour footprints around the kitchen, covering every inch of floor tile.

Stepping into this house was like entering into another life; the childhood he wished he had lived. Mandy looked unconcerned over the antics of the twins, nicknamed 'The Chaos Team.' She had joked before that Henry and Hadley were washable and she saw the messes they made mostly as learning explorations. When he was their age, almost three years old, his mother had made him scrub his own fingerprints off the fridge, her hand suffocating his, her voice drowning out his crying. His mother hadn't really liked kids, but she came from a time and place where women were expected to be wives and wives were expected to have children. She had only given birth to one and she had made a point of telling all the neighbours that Gavin should count for at least two. He understood now that she had used his alleged bad behaviour as an excuse not to have more kids. Most of the time Gavin had kept to himself. His dad enjoyed baseball and tinkering with their two cars. He could remember watching his dad play on his company's soccer team and baseball team. Gavin had played T-ball, but he spent most of his time sitting on the bench. His dad was busy; weeknights he didn't usually come home in time for dinner and he spent weekends in the garage. Gavin had snuck into the garage a couple of times to watch his father work and listen to the game on the radio with him, but when his mother saw his pants covered in grease she screamed that unless his dad was going to start doing laundry, Gavin should stay out.

He opened the door and walked inside as warm air enveloped his body. 'Hello', he said.

'Gavin!' Henry and Hadley ran over and hugged his legs.

'Thank goodness, you're finally here', Mandy grinned, wiping her hands on her apron, and reaching over the kids to give him a hug.

'How's it going?' Gavin noticed even Mandy's long eyelashes had traces of flour on them.

'Good. Hadley and Henry, if you let Gavin wash your hands and feet off, you can make the sauce with him.'

'Do you guys want to be my helpers?' Gavin turned the kitchen sink on and fiddled with the water temperature until it was just right. Henry and Hadley were laughing and making flour handprints on his jeans and sweater. He lifted Henry up and stuck his chubby little feet under the water. Henry giggled as Gavin squirted soap on his feet and washed the flour off. Hadley was much lighter but she wiggled all around, and it was hard to get her hands and feet under the water.

After everyone was dried off, he opened the cans of tomatoes and let the twins take turns dumping them in the bowl and stirring. Hopefully the recipe didn't require exact quantities, he thought, because they both wanted to add salt and pepper with the special measuring teaspoon set. Mandy finished frying the vegetables and prepared the fish. Finally the four of them assembled everything into a big casserole dish and put it in the oven.

'Henry and Hadley, go tell Daddy that dinner will be ready in fifteen minutes.'

They raced towards the coatroom to get to the back door of the garage.

Mandy smiled at Gavin. The white handprints on his pants were occasionally intersected by red streaks of tomato sauce. 'Thanks for making the sauce with the kids. It was a big help.'

Mandy poured three glasses of wine and handed one to him. She was looking at him intently, her blue eyes appearing almost curious. He looked down at his glass and took a sip of the wine. It was a Riesling, one of his favourites.

'So, what's so important that I am here alone?'

Henry, Hadley, and Jack spilled through the door. Jack was chasing them, shouting, 'I'm going to catch you and tickle you!'

The twins ran squealing with delight and hid behind Mandy. Jack tossed his football shirt towards the laundry room revealing a white t-shirt beneath, and he began washing his hands. Mandy walked over and stood on her tiptoes to kiss Jack's cheek. 'Did the mechanic do what you asked?'

'Looks like it.' He easily picked her up and kissed her on the lips, her feet dangling a foot above the ground.

Gavin ignored the display of affection and lit the candles and distributed plates and glasses around the table. He knew where everything was and Mandy wasn't the kind of person who cared which side the fork went on. There was always a lot going on with the two kids, and she cared first and foremost that they were happy and not getting into trouble. Since Victoria had left Gavin, he had a lot of time on his hands and Jack and Mandy appreciated having him around. Gavin and Jack had designed and built the patio outside last summer, and he had helped Mandy hang the Christmas lights off the roof. At the twins' birthday he had been in charge of retrieving wayward balloons from the ceiling.

By the time the table was set and the kids were corralled, the steaming casserole was ready to come out of the oven. 'Let's eat,' said Mandy.

The five of them moved towards the table. Jack sat at the head of the table flanked by Hadley and Henry. Gavin and Mandy sat on the opposite sides of the kids and across from one another.

'Cheers,' said Hadley and clunked her sippy cup against Gavin's wine glass.

'Cheers,' repeated Henry and they all knocked glasses and sippy cups in the middle of the table. Gavin watched as Jack briefly locked his eyes with Mandy's as Jack reached to clink his glass against hers.

'It looks like the tile store I pass on the way here is having a big sale,' said Gavin.

'Excellent, maybe we can get some ideas for a new bathroom?' said Mandy.

'Are you guys thinking of remodelling?'

'Always, ' Jack smiled. 'Would you be up for lending me a hand with another project?'

'Sure, the patio came out great.'

Jack liked the idea of doing it 'himself,' but Gavin had found that really Jack enjoyed overseeing home projects more than using a hammer. Gavin didn't mind helping out. He found it satisfying to accomplish something visible, like switch out a sink or recaulk a bathroom tub. Fixing things was the one activity that brought up fond memories of his father. His father had guided his hand on the roller, showing him how to paint without leaving drips or streaks.

Hadley climbed from her chair into Gavin's lap. She smelled of baby shampoo. 'I'm not hungry, let's go play trains.'

'Hadley, Gavin's still eating. Why don't you come sit by Mommy?'

'It's yummy, Hadley. You should eat some more,' said Gavin.

'I want to sit on Gavin's lap too,' said Henry.

'Let Gavin finish eating first. If you're both done with dinner, why don't you go play?' said Mandy

'Okay,' they scampered off to the playroom.

Mandy refilled everyone's wine glasses. 'Can I get either of you more fish?' She served both Jack and Gavin and sat back down.

'We're thinking of having a third child,' said Mandy.

Gavin picked up his wine glass. 'That's wonderful, congratulations. Is this your way of asking for my help to convert the guest suite into a baby room?'

'We're not there yet,' said Jack.

'Thanks Gavin for the offer, but first we have another favour to ask of you. Your friendship these past years has meant a lot to all of us, Jack, Hadley, Henry, and especially me.' Mandy paused.

'Gav, would you consider donating sperm?'

'Excuse me?' Gavin didn't understand. 'What? Why?'

'We would like you to consider donating sperm to us, of course.'

'But Jack, you have two kids?' Was this a joke? He looked to Mandy for help.

'We're serious Gavin,' said Mandy. 'We would like you to be the biological father of our third child.'

'Why me, why not Jack?' He pushed his chair back from the table; the two of them were both staring at him. Gavin needed more space. 'If you already have two kids, there must be some way to have a third. I'm sure if you saw a specialist ...'

'We've seen a specialist,' said Mandy. She began twirling her wine glass.

'Look, I think I've taken too many hits on the field,' said Jack. 'We got lucky the first time around, but now my sperm are too defective. They're still swimming though.'

Gavin blushed and pushed his hand against his forehead attempting to remove the image of disfigured sperm out of his mind. He hated when Jack talked like this. Was this how he comforted his patients, by relating everything to sports? He rubbed his sweaty palms on the napkin on his lap.

'We've carefully considered all the options and we would really be honoured if you would be the biological father,' said Mandy.

Gavin could feel sweat dripping down his back. What did it mean to be a biological father? Would he feel responsible if there was something wrong with the baby? Would he be to blame if the baby became a teenager who cut classes to drink and smoke cigarettes? Outside, the wind had picked up and the snow was blowing all around. He watched to see if the wind might die down, maybe then he could make some sense out of the turmoil in his own head.

'Why me?' he asked.

'You look like you could be my scrawny kid brother,' said Jack.

'I don't know about that.'

'You're healthy. You work out, right?'

'Yes.'

'I know you don't play now, but did you ever play football as a kid?'

'No.'

'Did you play any team sports?'

'T-ball.'

'In any case, you're smart. You have to be to work with Mandy.'

'I guess,' said Gavin.

'Mandy and I've discussed this and made up our minds. You're our pick, Gav.'

Gavin slowly drank from his wine glass. He was 'their pick,' as if this was a grade school gym class. He would have thought Jack would pick him last.

'Gavin,' Mandy stopped twirling her glass and looked up. 'You are an honest, caring person and a good friend. We're positive we couldn't find a better donor.'

Gavin felt his chest tighten, anxiety flooding his lungs. Mandy was serious. He coughed, but the unrelenting itch in his throat would not subside.

'Are you choking on a fish bone?' asked Mandy.

'No,' he continued coughing.

Hadley returned. 'Are you sick Gavin? Do you need to go to the hospital?'

Hadley patted him on the back with her little hand. Gavin drank some more wine. This whole thing was sick. 'Thanks, Hadley.'

'Do you want to play trains now?

Before he could answer, Jack cut him off. 'Hadley, we haven't finished dinner yet. Go play with Henry.'

They watched Hadley run back to the playroom. More than anything, Gavin wanted to follow her and push the little engines around and forget all of this. He felt dizzy and swallowed another sip of wine hoping it might dull the waves of apprehension rolling through him. He had taken a shower before coming tonight, but now the neck of his t-shirt was stuck to his skin. He looked at Mandy; she didn't meet his gaze. She was playing with her necklace, her wedding band and engagement ring sparkling in the light.

Jack stood up grabbed a folder and placed it in front of Gavin. The folder was white with *Fertility Centre* printed in big black letters, underlined. Underneath it read: *Sperm Donation Basics.* 'Take a look,' said Jack, 'The medical process is quite straightforward, not invasive at all. We'll make it as easy for you as possible.'

Gavin's head felt so heavy he slumped down so he could rest it against the back of the chair. Jack seemed to be handling Gavin the same way he would treat a patient with a broken arm, but this was a big deal, not in any way easy. If he did this, would he really be considered a father? It would be his kid, or at least half his kid, even if the child didn't know. Would Jack be the kind of father he had craved? He felt ill, and he thought he might have to vomit.

Gavin read slowly aloud trying to make this feel real: 'sperm donation basics.' He couldn't open the folder.

'It wouldn't take much effort on your part,' said Jack. 'You would first need to undergo a blood test and have a trial run at the doctor's office. Then when Mandy's cycle was right you would have to go back. The room they provide you with is quite nice, there's even a DVD player.'

The thought of touching the controls of such a DVD player made him want to gag. Gavin always used a paper towel to touch the handle of the men's room at work. 'Excuse me, I have to go to the bathroom.' He concentrated on standing up and putting one foot in front of the other. He hoped he was walking normally as he crossed the ten feet to the door of the downstairs bathroom. He closed the door, turned the water on, put the lid down on the toilet and sat down burying his head in his hands: defective sperm. These were words that he had never expected to hear uttered at dinner in this house. He had always wanted to be a father, but he hadn't imagined it beginning and ending with a plastic cup. This shouldn't be happening. He had expected to be married to Victoria by now and thinking of having his own children. He would have tried to be the father he had wanted as a kid, patient and involved. The type of father that built elaborate tracks for the toy trains, and blanket forts to sleep in, and pretended to be a wild horse as he carried his kids on his back. He wanted to be there to kiss his kids when they fell down and comfort them after they woke up from a nightmare. He wanted to be the father he had craved. Maybe his dad would have been this person had he not died when Gavin was six.

Why did Jack and Mandy want his sperm? Wouldn't it be easier to go with an anonymous donor? Did they think Gavin would make a good father? He doubted that Jack looked much further than Gavin's outer shell. Gavin knew people thought him attractive: tall, thin, dark hair, bright blue eyes. He could likely pass as Jack's brother physically. Mandy knew him better. She was candid and sincere and the person at work whom he trusted the most. She could tell if something was bothering him. She wouldn't take no as an answer so once he had admitted to her that sometimes he felt awkward in social situations. At a meeting or group lunch, he would often look over and she would meet his eyes and smile. Afterwards, if he was obsessing about something she would tell him that he was cheerful and fine, and make a comment like, 'didn't you notice the Managing Partner couldn't stop talking to you?' A while ago she had recommended he try Prozac. 'Jack has been on it for years,' she had said. 'His sister thinks it has made him more selfish, but at least he's happier.' After tonight's chain of events he could see where Jack's sister might be coming from. He was spending too long in the bathroom, but he didn't care. He could hear whispering outside and Henry and Hadley began knocking on the door. 'Gavin, are you going pee pee on the potty?'

'Kids, let Gavin be,' said Mandy.

He could hear the television turn on in the other room and the kids drifted away. He wanted to have kids. What if this was his only chance? His sperm could fertilize an egg, creating the miracle of life. That would be something, an undeniable contribution to future generations.

There was no doubt in his mind that Mandy was a great mother. She would do anything for her kids. He knew she budgeted money carefully so she could work part-time and take Hadley and Henry to music, art, and gymnastics classes. Gavin didn't mind if she occasionally went home early when her nanny was worried about a bumped head or a possible fever. Mandy would make up the time after the kids went to bed. Gavin had never seen her lose her temper at home or at work, even when Henry screamed, 'Mummy I hate you.' Gavin's mother would have slapped him across the face, but Mandy just said 'timeout'.

He didn't know Jack as well. Jack was sweet and affectionate to Mandy and the kids whenever Gavin was around. However, Jack had convinced Mandy to move out of the city, even though she had mentioned that she would have rather stayed close to work in the neighbourhood where most of her friends were. She did agree it was the right move in the long run. Gavin didn't know if Jack was the kind of father who would throw his son a football a thousand times even if he hated football. Would Jack let his kids follow their own passions and not resent them if they did?

Gavin stood up, flushed the toilet for effect, and splashed water on his face to try to make sense of his thoughts. He opened the door. Jack and Mandy were sitting in the exact same spots waiting for him. He concentrated on walking back to the table. He sat down and flipped the folder over.

'It's a lot to think about,' Gavin said.

'I know it's a lot to ask, Gavin.' Mandy took a sip of her wine.

'What's your concern?' asked Jack.

'Would you tell the kid?'

'Would we tell the kid what, Gav?'

'That I'm the father.'

'You wouldn't be the father, I would.'

'I mean the biological father.'

'I don't think that's important.'

'I guess it depends on how you see it.' Gavin looked at Mandy. She was watching the snow fall outside.

'We would raise the child as ours, but you could still be part of his or her life,' she said.

'How? It will be our child, the same as Henry and Hadley,' said Jack.

'Well, Gavin is part of their lives now. He sees them almost every week.'

Gavin thought about this. Did he want to become 'Uncle Gavin,' invited for holidays and birthdays with the rest of the relatives? He could see his son or daughter grow, but he would be powerless, essentially an absentee father. Would he feel a connection to this child beyond what he felt for Henry and Hadley that would make it hard for him to play this role? Would he recognise himself in the child? Could he quietly stand aside?

'Yes, but I will be this child's father,' said Jack.

'You will be the child's father, but Gavin will be the biological father. Even if no-one knows it except us, it's understandable that Gavin might want to feel connected.'

'What do you mean by connected?' Jack glared at Mandy. Her face didn't register his anger. A phone began to ring. Jack pulled his cell phone from his pocket and checked the number. 'You'll have to excuse me for a moment.' He walked up the stairs.

'I feel connected to Hadley and Henry,' said Gavin.

'I know you do, Gavin, and I think it would be impossible not to feel an attachment to a biological child even if you weren't on the official birth certificate.' Mandy turned to look outside. Gavin wondered where her thoughts were wandering. She knew a lot about his unhappy childhood and that he hated spending holidays with his own mother. Was this her way of making him part of their family?

She picked up her plate and walked into the kitchen. Gavin gathered his plate, then Jack's and the kids' plates and carried them towards the sink. He would like to become a permanent part of their family. Maybe being 'Uncle Gavin' would be okay. Maybe this third child could give him license to love them as if they were all part of extended family. Gavin thought Mandy would allow this, but would Jack? Was Jack hiding his true feelings about the seriousness of biological fatherhood? He was a doctor and it would be clear to him that this child undeniably would have Gavin's genes interwoven with Mandy's. What if he had Gavin's smile? Would Jack notice this? Would Mandy?

Mandy had her back to him. He could see small handprints on her dress where the apron hadn't covered. He placed the stacked plates next to hers and watched the water run over them erasing the traces of the meal.

'Mandy?'

She shrugged her shoulders.

'You okay?' Gavin lightly touched her shoulder with his hand.

She spun around and buried her head against his chest, her arms tightly around him. 'I'm so sorry Gavin. It's a difficult decision. You'll need time to think.'

He felt she had collapsed into him. He hugged her tightly and then worked his arms to her shoulders and pushed her to arm's length. The tears streaming down her face highlighted her nose and pink lips. He felt her vulnerability, and it made his chest twinge where the tears spotted his shirt. He let her fall back into his arms.

'Gavin, we would love your child, our child.' Her head rested on his heart. 'We thought about this for a long time and Jack and I both agreed on you.' He pushed her back to arm's length, and reclaimed his hands from her shoulders. 'I'll understand if it is too much for you though, it is asking a lot. Most people don't associate having a child with a plastic cup. I wouldn't let it end with that.'

Gavin took a deep breath and buried his hands in his pockets.

Jack walked into the kitchen and snapped his phone closed. 'Gav, the plastic cup isn't really that bad.'

'It just doesn't fit with my idea of fatherhood.'

'I understand it's a sterile way to conceive a child. I had a bit of a hard time with it the first time around, but it was the only way.'

'Jack, it's more than that.'

'Gavin, we would want you to stay a part of our lives. Even though Jack would be the father, we would still welcome you. There can never be too much love.' The tear streaks from earlier were still visible across Mandy's face as she smiled.

'I'll do it, but I won't go to the clinic.'

'Gav, you have to go to the clinic, you can't donate at home. It needs to be sterile, they need to process the sperm.'

'That's not what I meant. If I'm going to do this, I would want to do it naturally.'

Mandy's blue eyes were cloudy, he couldn't see into them. Jack looked astonished, 'Are you saying you want to have sex with my wife?'

'If you want me to make a baby, then yes.' Gavin knew it was an outlandish request, but his life currently was shadowed by isolation and rejection. Mandy seemed capable for accepting him as he was. If they were willing to grant him this request he hoped this one act and the child that followed could secure his place in the family forever.

'Gav, I think of you as my brother. Let's stick to the clinic.'

Gavin turned towards Mandy. He was happy to see that she didn't look horrified. He didn't want to hurt her or her family, Gavin just wanted to secure his place in it. Mandy met his eyes. The corners of her mouth turned up slightly. He knew that it would be okay; she understood why he wanted to share this moment with her. His footprints would be left behind.

Leeroy

Matthew Cai

'I'm a nice bastard, aren't I?'
Leeroy sings loud praises, echoing
his colleagues' appeasing smiles,
moulded from the mouths of Steve, Lex and Jes:
an electric screwdriver, wash sponge and waste bin
in a system of systems.
And within the daily din of our large garage factory,
my benevolent envy overhears
this masterly raillery –
and we work; cleaning, fixing,
grinding – to gentrify these motorcars
that belong to middle class millionaires.

Small Gods

Christina Guo

You like to think you chose this fate.

Perhaps in the space between falling into white and waking up, a part of you had reached through the nothingness and seen it for what it was. Maybe, as your last mortal memories were shed off you like a cicada shell, you had closed your eyes, concentrated really hard into the dark, and heard the question. Maybe you had weighed your options on your tongue, and replied, 'I accept.'

Whatever had happened, you had emerged on top of a cloud, the world above flat and calm despite the misty foundation it laid on. Lying on your back, sunlight on your chest, the sticky, gleaming strands of eternity coating your being like amber. Your time stopped at forever.

Clotho had been waiting for you, her face youthful but with an ancient kind of sympathy lining the edges of her smile. She sat with you, watching the world turn navy then inky black, and answered your questions one by one with calm patience. By the end, the knowledge of what you have to do was cut into your bones. Your questions, really, boiled down to one. '*Why?*'

'Everyone questions that when they begin,' she told you. 'Why us? Will more of us appear? Will we ever remember our mortal lives? Is there an alternative? Is this a reward or punishment?' Her voice trailed off, but you had pressed on. 'So which is it? A reward or a punishment?'

Clotho took a while to reply. 'It's a job,' she had said finally, but there was an ancient sort of wistfulness to her face. 'Maybe you're the one who has to decide.'

People's futures are chains, fine as spider silk, tied to their arms, necks and legs, fading in and out of sight as the light changes. Like the strings held by a balloon-seller, they wave as people walk. You stand in the city street, feeling a slight tremble in your being as people walk through you, and watch as chains come loose from all directions and fall to the ground.

'An abandoned future,' Clotho said, bending down to pick up a chain. You do the same and suddenly you were looking at a middle-aged man standing on the train, doing up the cuffs of his slate grey suit. 'That was the train he could have caught if he had run from his office,' Clotho said, and you watched as the thread crumbled in your palm. 'But he decided to walk.'

You have an eternity to wander through houses, streets, and side alleyways, picking up chains you didn't get to witness being detached. Potential futures dying because of acts of nature, choices and random occurrences of chance. The only thing you know for certain is that there are no rules, and no formulas.

The singer is young and ready to take on the world. The people around him frown, pointing to his school marks, begging him to reconsider: consider your throat, consider your future, consider what everyone else will *say*. He shakes his head, quietly determined, and the chain falls from his arm and onto the ground. You pick it up to see a future where he's in his thirties, without time for the music he loves so much, lost among the sea of others. You look at the young boy before you and hope for the best. Five years later, you watch him get by on three hours of sleep a day, memorise scripts and interviewers' names in his spare time, call airports his second home. You watch him sing to a screaming ocean of fans, silhouetted in rainbow stage lights, every note and beat of music affirming the determination and joy still in his eyes. *No regrets.*

When you appear in the dancer's room, she has an acceptance letter for university in one hand (the final product of long nights, a bookshelf of painstakingly written notes, and falling asleep over her textbooks) and an invitation to join a large dance company in the other. You're not sure what to think as she places the dance company invitation in her drawer, to be tucked away forever. The chain of that future detaches itself surprisingly quickly from her wrist. Five years later, her graduation certificate still sits proudly on her shelf. She's seeing the world, living new dreams, and she's happy.

In the future she left behind, she is middle-aged and still favouring her not-quite-healed right leg, swallowing back a mix of pride and regret as she watches her students dance on the stage that she left too early.

It's a hard job, no-one argues with that. Even the God of Lost Socks has an occasional prayer thrown exasperatedly at him from exasperated mothers and people who rifle desperately through their drawers, their eyes on the clock. You're the God of Abandoned Futures. You don't get prayers, only regrets, if anything.

You feel it most keenly when you're standing in a crowded bus looking at the soul mates. Maybe the Irony God is feeling particularly vindictive because they're sitting next to each other and this is not the regular bus for either of them. You never *know* what the future is before it detaches itself from the person for you to pick up and by that time, whatever future you see is already a past tense, a lost opportunity. Even without knowing, you can tell they would be happy together.

A resolution is forming in one of them to just *say something*. But the moment passes in the lurch of the brakes as they arrive at the bus stop. One of them stands up, steps out, and you can taste the resigned, slightly bitter tang of regret in both of their hearts, and a small spark of hope. *Next time I'll say hello.* Later. Next time.

It's almost enough for you to want to be real, and press the chain of their intertwined futures into their unsuspecting hands. But they will never meet again. The chain of what could have been lingers a second longer before it breaks softly into your hands, and, just for a moment, you feel like you might cry.

Most abandoned futures are small enough to pick up in handfuls as they are littered across the ground; quick, split-second decisions people make every day. The extra ten minutes the man would have spent waiting if he hadn't run for that bus, or the beef baguette that the teenager could have bought, but she chose chicken instead. Their tiny chain links crumble into silver dust that you scatter in the wind, unnoticed and unmourned. Then there is 'I hate you!' the screech of car brakes (too late) and a mother and son argument that was never finished.

You're there as the boy sits, face blank in his black clothes, a ghost among the gentle platitudes of friends and distant relatives. He replays the argument over and over in his head, and the chain of the future that should have crumbled stays fresh around his neck, sharp and cutting in his grief.

He's still wearing it, an Ancient Mariner with his albatross, when you find him again. His face has been weathered by time, with loss, love, happiness, grief and everything in between etched into the lines on his skin. Only when he closes his eyes for the last time does the silver chain gently slide from his neck, like a farewell.

You hesitate for a long time, not sure whether you should pick the chain up. When you do, the chain is warm; things held inside one's heart always are. You close your eyes and look into the abandoned future. 'I'm sorry for yelling at you,' the young boy says.

'It's okay,' his mother replies. This time, his small, grudging, hopeful smile is the last thing she sees.

Sometimes, though, the most banal moments are the saddest and, somehow, the most terrifying to deal with. You're standing in a messy university student dorm, in the middle of the sleepy remnants of a Friday night get-together. The car is new and the boy is eighteen, carefree and confident.

'Hey, we're going to race home, you in?' Even here, you can smell the sickly sweetness of alcohol clinging to his friend. You watch the boy look up; take in the casual slouch of his shoulders, the careless flick of his fingers as he plays with the fabric of the sofa and the haziness of the alcohol seeping into his eyes.

So often, you wish you could know the outcome before it happened. The two chains glint around his wrists. You hold your breath. 'Nah, I'm going to sleep it off. I've got a nine am lecture tomorrow,' he says, closing his eyes and slumping into the sofa. 'Damn, that's tough. See you later, man.'

In the lifetime you pick up, you see shattered windscreen gleaming on the concrete, a group of friends bursting into the hospital room, and a family fighting back their tears as the coffin is lowered into the ground.

In this lifetime, the boy laughs, sleeps and lives on.

Stuck – *Kokkai Ng*

Ruby Li's Australian Dream

Wang Zi

Ruby Li always shows her first-time guests around her home at Concord. She lives in a red-brick house that enjoys serene views of the bay. Walking in the nearby park Li casts occasional glances at her attic through the leaves and bushes, as if she is keeping an eye on the house in case it disappears.

'My Buddha face [referring to her broad forehead and chin, and ready smile] wrinkled a lot these years. It still doesn't reveal the hardships I have been through,' she says as she smiles, her golden bifocals resting on pierced ears.

Standing in a pair of chocolate-coloured boots with a flowery sweater and brownish hair, Li is not the typical image of a sixty-five-year-old Chinese woman. Most of her peers in China have long since retired but Li still bustles around, regularly flying between Australia and China as the Coordinator of China Liaison of St Paul's Grammar School. She keeps a tight schedule, meeting partners, initiating exchange programs, and dealing with emails and phone calls every day.

Ruby Li's story in Sydney began twenty-five years ago when, at the age of forty, she became the first Australian visa applicant from the city of Shaoxing, Zhejiang province. She arrived in 1987 with two things: a leather case of clothes, and a wallet with $30 – the maximum foreign currency a departing Chinese citizen was allowed by a country just embracing the global market.

'Looking for anything that pays', was among the first sentences she threw at a friend at the airport. She soon questioned leaving everything behind. She worked as a factory labourer wrapping boxes, a job she would have normally frowned upon as a trained medical school lecturer.

'Are you alright? You are crying?' asked a fellow Chinese worker, handing her a handkerchief.

'No, nothing. I am just a bit overwhelmed.'

'But you made your own decision to come here?'

'Yes.'

'Then forget what you were. You will be alright.'

'Thank you. What did you do before you came here?' asked Li, trying to know more about her co-worker.

'I was a university professor.'

Ever since then, Li has not shed any tears.

She thought her bachelor degree would land her better jobs but, as she only had a two-year record of university education in China, her transcript and graduation certificate was not recognised by the administrators in Australia.

These events did not help convince her she had made the right choice. Sitting on the platform of Central Station Li could hear a traumatising echo hovering in her head, over and over again: 'Long live the invincible socialist nation!'

In 1964 eighteen-year-old Li enrolled at Jilin University, one of the top institutions in China. She was majoring, in an era where Russian was the only foreign language in the country, in an unusual subject, English Literature.

Orientation was held on campus in a Soviet-style auditorium, the head of the school preaching that the country was expected to join the United Nations in five years, the graduation year for these young elite of the republic. Li was excited at the prospect of becoming a future diplomat, interpreter, or policymaker as China integrated into the international community. For the next two years, Li hardly enjoyed leisure but worked hard, reading English and listening to BBC News programs.

The fifth of August 1966 was the beginning of Li's roller-coaster ride of fate. Just as she was about to become a university junior the Cultural Revolution started to crash across the country. The national education system ceased operating, making way for political campaigns. Her campus soon became a parade spot where many liberal-minded scholars were publicly condemned and humiliated.

Li, along with millions of other youths, dressed up in military uniform with a red armband and boarded the train for Beijing. There she attended an unprecedented million-people-parade at Tiananmen Square, where Chairman Mao was to greet the 'glorious red guards'.

After idling on campus for three years, her placement year finally arrived in 1969. It was a year in which she had been promised a bright future, but the revolution made another dramatic turn. College students became the next target to be reformed. Military officers took over the campuses. Those students who used to condemn their teachers were to be 're-educated' by soldiers, peasants, and workers before they were sent to rural areas for further reformation.

'Crazy,' reflected Li sitting on the train from Central Station. She could not help having a flashback, remembering a daughter pointing her fingers at her own parents, cuffed, at a public gathering, accusing them of betraying the party by expressing different political views at home.

But her thrilling retrospect of the frenzy years was soon diluted by the greater anxiety of her dimming prospects as a forty-year-old labourer in a foreign land.

Determined to be a teacher again she studied a certificate course for Asian language teaching at the University of New South Wales in 1988. But without any local teaching experience she traded her application forms for the same pile of rejection letters. So she started working as a stand-by Chinese teacher at various schools, hoping to get some scraps of classes in exchange for cash. Teaching three to four different classes in different suburbs was demanding. Every evening she lay down on the floor, exhausted. Still, busy days were much better than the holiday weeks, when the cash flow simply dried up. Many times she pleaded with her landlord for later deposit of rent.

Three years dragged on. She rarely called her friends in China. There was nothing to tell them.

At the beginning of 1992, in order to gain support for his plan to set up a compulsory Chinese language course, Dr Stephen Codrington, the principal of St Paul's Grammar School in Penrith, delivered a report on China. His research and vision showed that China, with its double-digit GDP growth over the last decade, was on its way to become a major economy and regional power. Many parents who had previously ridiculed the plan were convinced, believing that Chinese language teaching could give an edge to their children in the future.

Soon after Dr Codrington's report Li came across a small advertisement in the paper: 'two Chinese teachers needed, Penrith, full-time'. Li usually skipped full-time job advertisements, because rejections had been her only reply through all the years, but on impulse she put the forms for the full time job into the mailbox.

Lying on the floor after another long day, Li was brought to her feet by the answering machine; a voice offered her an interview.

At the age of forty-five, for the first time, she was offered a chance at a full-time job.

Just hours after the interview Li was peeling potatoes, listening to her answering machine. The last message was from St Paul's. She'd been given the job. With the peeler still in her trembling hand and a potato rolling around on the floor, she slowly crouched down, tears spotting her apron.

After this, life got on the express lane. Soon she took out a mortgage on a house in Lidcombe, and she now often made phone calls back to China, updating those back home with the changes: people's craze about big screen TVs, multi gear bicycles, and the Sony Walkman. She always ended the call with 'if you come to Sydney, stay in my house, it's big enough'.

Because of China's booming economy Li's school saw the prospect of cooperating with their Chinese counterparts in language teaching, and Li was assigned to set up a partnership.

On one of those business trips in 1999 Li, who was staying in a grand hotel room in Beijing's booming business district, was awakened by a dream: feeling herself tumbling into a dingy pool of greasily filthy water, struggling.

It is the same nightmare that has invaded her sleep for over thirty years, since her youth during the Cultural Revolution. 'If I have to go back to that place again, I would rather kill myself,' she swears.

The 'place' is the backdrop of Li's nightmare. When she was sent to reformation during the Cultural Revolution her destination was a remote village near forestland on China's northern border. The village was a harsh place, where the temperature dropped to minus thirty – forty degrees throughout its six-month winter.

She was not alone there, 120 top university graduates lined up with her for allocation by the local official.

'You studied Fluid Dynamics?'

'Yes,' answered a male student from Tsinghua University.

'Fluid, uh? Go to water company, it matches your occupation. And you three speak bird's language?'

'Yes,' answered Li and other two female students, who majored in Japanese and French.

'Not sure what you can do. Let's draw lots, it's only fair.'

Li was sent to the public bathing pool to work as a cleaner. She was twenty-three. Residents went to the bathing facility every two weeks, one week for females and another week for males. Due to the slippery floors Li often fell down into the filthy water where hundreds of people bathed.

For the following seven years, like everyone in the country, Li recited Chairman Mao's quotes aloud before breakfast and again before sleep. She married her college boyfriend, whose parents both committed suicide in the political campaign, believing her life would end in the village.

In 1976, when she had long adapted to the life in the far north of China, Chairman Mao passed away. Deng Xiaoping came to power as the party leader and pushed reform. As quickly as it had started the ten-year revolution ended.

'Many people didn't understand me leaving the country when things were getting better in the years of reform,' recalled Li from the couch at her home in Concord. But the blow that scattered her expectation for a better life was her husband filing for divorce in 1987, her parents having passed away years earlier.

'Suddenly I realised that I was all alone. I lost everything. I was in despair with the thought of not having roots anymore,' said Li. 'I had a strong impulse to start all over again when I still got the guts to do so.'

Now living in Sydney, Li's traumatised experience in China's most dramatic years has gradually dissolved, faded and eroded by time. Instead she is excited, the Chinese people and country becoming rich a stark contrast to when she was in the village where the endless boundary of forest meets the horizon.

Her flashback is suddenly interrupted by a phone call. It is from the father of a Chinese student who has just been expelled from her school. Closing the call, she shakes her head. 'Now Chinese really is becoming rich. The boy's father is a coal mine owner in Shanxi province. He thinks that he can take care of anything by throwing cash. But things don't work that way here.'

Untitled
(To come home to endless homes …)

Hugo Branley

To come home to endless homes,
To the blue call of forgotten nooks
Hung in the trees like a banner.

In the blue scent of forgotten boughs
The last is forgotten, old arrayed
And the grass gives slightly underfoot;

Rest still and afraid under eyelids, or
Each step could be called a homecoming.

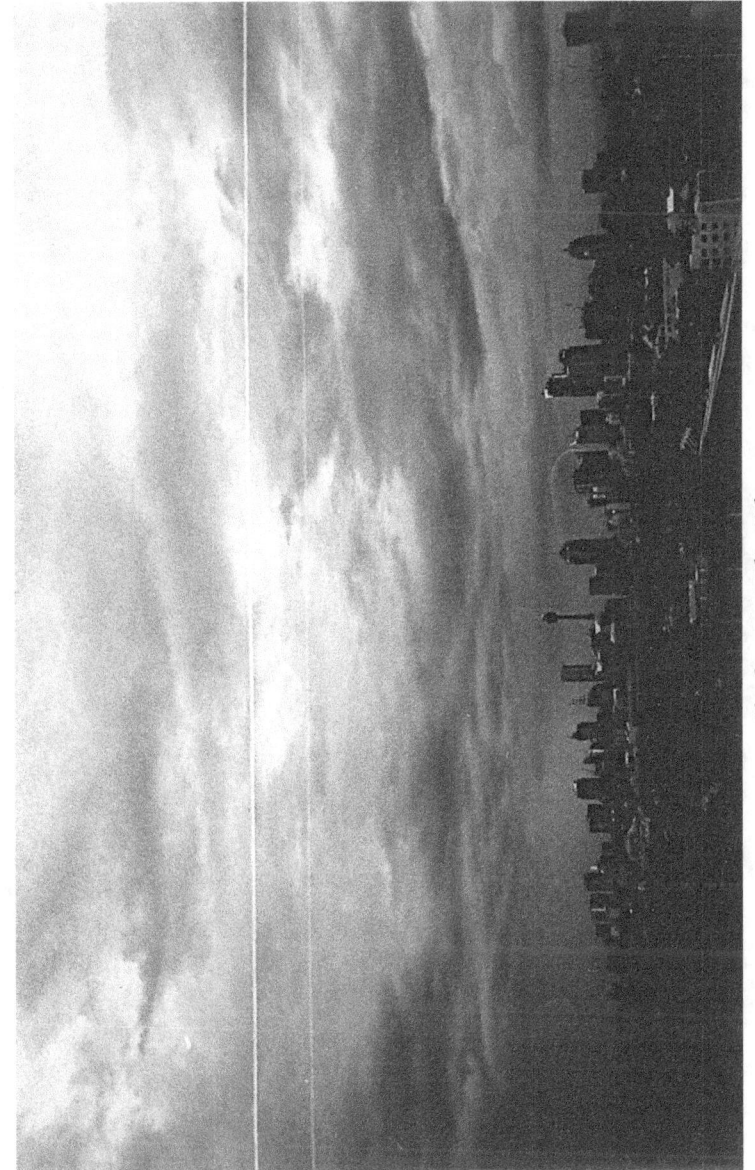

Shadows – Lidia Nikonova

Smokescreen Silhouettes

Celeste Moore

I

sparkling stars above darkened cars
windows fogged up with the
sound of their bodies
together, screaming
'I don't love you'

II

Your breath is warm as it slips down and
Out, my gasping, grasping throat, filled with your
Unknown scent – more than I can withstand.

In and out it weaves, the smoke I abhor
Never again will I let it hold me
Tie its thin, waify arms around my waist,
Open wide and swallow, lest I get free.
Xanthic eyes trace the body they can't taste
Ignoring each call-sign of self-abuse.
Chastely, carefully, as you labour over
And over, I drain you of your muse.
Tell me, I whisper to my godless lover,
Emerald eyes lighting up my night skies.

'May you be happy,' she softly cries.
Envious eyes become your jealous spies.

III

This smokescreen is my penance
For the nights spent mapping
Spindly silhouettes against
The grey of the sky.

This scent will never leave
The windswept moor of my mind
Where every touch and every word
Has its own locked room.

Maybe this is the madness
You warned me about, laughing
As you handed me an aluminium can
Full of dreams and promises
That neither of us could deliver.

Those shared breaths and
Cigarette-end hopes
Kept me thinking that the madness
Was buried just under our fingernails
Waiting for the DNA test.

The bright lights and the dark nights
Walking the streets alone have changed me.

I have a confession:
The madness never existed.
It was just as pretty a story
As you were.

Quarter After One

Kevin Caucher

It was a quarter after one. The crowd was coming down, and the disco-esque music of the bar changed to the latest single of Lady Antebellum. You quite liked the country act so you relaxed, leaning against a stool behind the bar.

You looked to your right, the usual spot where this guy Cliff always sat. He spotted you. 'Vince, what time is it?'

'Quarter past one.'

He nodded, then pulled out his cell phone and dialled a number. 'Hi Phil,' Cliff said.

You loved your job. Being a bartender gave you the opportunity to observe people, and the occasional really nice tips was an added bonus.

The latest target of your observation was Cliff.

He was a regular. He was mostly here on Saturdays. You spotted him the first time when he gave you a big tip. He had ordered three drinks that night already when he asked you for a fourth Mojito. He seemed sober enough. Yet you still reminded him of the three he had.

'Well, then get me a ginger ale instead, please, uh …'

'Vince.'

'Yeah. Thank you Vince.' He shoved a bill into your hand. 'And keep the change.'

'But …' There was too much change for a tip.

'Keep it.' He waved you away. 'Now get me the ginger ale. I'm Cliff, by the way.'

The first encounter intrigued you. Cliff seemed only as old as a college student, or a grad student. Yet he had left you a big tip. You wondered about him and decided to observe him.

He had a variety of taste in cocktails. He was mostly a Long Island or Mojito guy, but he mixed it up sometimes with Blue Hawaii, or even just whisky on the rocks.

You had yet to really talk to him, except the first time and the ordering, but he seemed friendly enough to you. And he often asked you the time. You always wondered why he had to ask when he had his cell phone.

Some of the nights, Cliff would look almost happy. Those nights were the nights for Mojitos and Long Islands. He'd say hi to you and leave you to your business.

With those long drinks, he took sips, almost like he was savouring the spirit. He'd look around a bit, judging the crowd. Sometimes his eyes would stay on guys in their thirties, you had found, as if he was going to hit on them. However, Cliff only stared. He had this longing and needy look on him, but he would never leave his stool to go strike up a conversation.

Sometimes he'd get hit on by guys his age. Cliff would be very nice to them, keeping the conversation going, but from his body language you knew Cliff was only being polite. You found that very confusing. On one hand, he seemed really needy, looking around when no-one talked to him. On the other hand, he seemed oblivious to the flirting coming from guys his age. He appeared to have built an invisible wall to those men.

The only time Cliff would thrive was when a thirty-something man talked to him. That was a rare occasion, which made it rare to see him really smile, or even laugh. He enjoyed the conversations. Maybe it was a thing with older guys? However, the only thing he enjoyed with those 'older men' was the conversation. Whenever the others got physical or asked him to leave with them, Cliff would stop flirting abruptly, and lose interest all of a sudden.

Cliff was more like a tease, you found.

Some other nights, Cliff was really subdued. He'd come in the bar glumly and sit on his usual spot. At those times you'd get more of a curt order. Whisky. On the rocks. Double.

No matter how much alcohol you'd put in that glass, he'd been able to down the whole thing in one gulp, which often resulted in serious coughing. But he seemed not to mind.

At those times, you had also learnt to get a refill for him soon after he downed the first one. He would watch you pour the new glass with slightly misty eyes. He stared hard into the drink, as if there were a whole universe in there or he was looking for some kind of answers through it. You wondered what answers he was looking for. He seemed almost haunted. Sometimes his eyes got even mistier, almost teary. Maybe it's some bad memories, some terrible break-up? You never knew, but you felt awful for this poor guy.

Sometimes during those stares into the glass, other guys in the bar would hit on Cliff. Cliff looked nice to the eyes and you weren't surprised that he got hit on. However, the staring wouldn't get interrupted at all. He seemed to have entered a zone and just ignored those guys. Having seen it enough times, you learned to tell the poor suitor that there'd be no response.

You'd busy yourself with other customers at this point. There was nothing really to observe in Cliff except the long hard staring. It'd be another hour or so before he'd down the second one in several gulps. And then he'd take a third one, and after another long time of hard staring it would be about the time for the phone call.

The phone call. Whatever the mood Cliff was in, this is the one thing you could count on.

Around an hour and fifteen minutes after midnight, when the crowd died down, he would become sombre. He'd get your attention and ask you the time. After that, he'd take out his cell phone and make a call to 'Phil'.

He had done this every time he'd been here. And the dwindling crowd made it easy for you to access Cliff's side of conversation.

'Hi Phil.'

Cliff had drunk a lot this night, more than he would usually have. He had been moody and was already working on his fourth whisky on the rocks. Earlier that night this one guy kept bugging Cliff to talk. It annoyed Cliff so much that Cliff, for the first time, pushed the guy away, and would almost have made a scene if you hadn't intervened.

However, the conversation with 'Phil' wasn't unusual. Actually, it was the same every night.

'Well, nothing much. It's just that I missed you a lot and thought I'd call you and hear your voice.'

'I miss you Phil.'

'Uh-huh, I guess I'm a bit drunk.'

'Well, no-one's with me today. But I think I'll manage to get home. I wish you were here with me, though.'

'I know you had a long day. You're always busy. But anyways …'

'Yeah, I'll be fine.'

'I miss you Phil.'

'Yeah, I'll talk to you tomorrow.'

'Okay.'

Cliff cut the call and went back to staring his glass.

Normally by closing time, Cliff would have gone, but this night was apparently not a normal one. You found Cliff asleep with his hand holding tightly onto his cell phone. This had never happened before.

You walked towards his place at the bar and shook him, trying to wake him up. 'Hey bud, are you alright? The bar is closed.'

That seemed to wake him up, because Cliff's eyes shot open and he instinctively pulled his hand with the cell phone closer to him. However, he didn't seem to notice you, and he didn't respond to any of your words.

You tried again. 'Are you alright to get yourself home? The bar is closed. You want me to call you a taxi or do you want someone to come and take you home?'

That didn't work, though you notice Cliff start to murmur. You tried to listen by moving closer, but you couldn't make out what he was saying, but you recognise it to be a repeat of the same word.

Then an idea popped up. You thought you could call this Phil guy, and suddenly realised that was the name Cliff was murmuring. 'Cliff, you want me to call Phil?'

Not waiting for a reply, you tried to pry his fingers open. Cliff's eyes turned to you the moment he realized you were trying to get his cell phone, and you felt his fingers clutching tighter. 'What you doing?' Cliff slurred.

'I'm calling Phil.' Not getting a reply, you raised your voice. 'Phil, I'm calling Phil! To come and pick you up.' That name seemed to strike a chord in Cliff, and he loosened his hold.

You were kind of excited about calling Phil, since you had been observing Cliff for quite some time, and it would fulfil your curiosity if you could just talk to Phil or even see him.

You found the contact list on the cell phone. There was only this one contact named 'Phil'.

You dialled the number.

Your eyes widened.

'Sorry, the number you dialled is no longer available. Please try again later.'

So That You Know I Know

Daniel Zwi

We sit beside each other sometimes and I could swear that the hairs on our forearms actually rise until they're facing one another, reaching out like little feelers and straining to touch, like when you rub a balloon against your scalp and the hair sticks up: I'm almost certain that that happens when we're near. You must notice it too, Molly, don't be coy with me. You can feel your forearm fluff become erect when I'm next to you, but we've never acknowledged it to each other, God forbid. And our hair isn't the only thing standing erect when you're around Molly, I'm sorry to be so crass but it's true. I. Like. You.

We made out once but I think you were too drunk to remember. On that road trip to Brisbane, in a filthy motel in Pottsville after we got back from the tiny pub where the locals gave us dirty looks and later warmed to us and gave us hash. You sat on the bed next to me and our forearm hairs rose to meet, you looked at me and smiled with your eyes, 'this is what you've been waiting for, Dan, I know you so so well', and we kissed. Our friends were in the room at the time and they went outside for a cigarette when they saw us. You slid your hand down my stomach and touched my thing and I touched yours. And then you vomited onto the pillow twice. Sam said that we carried on kissing after that, and I was drunk too, but I don't think we did. The next day you had a terrible hangover and I told you that we'd kissed. You said that you had no recollection of it – you could have been lying to avoid awkwardness – and we laughed it off; we said it's okay, we're best friends. But I don't think you know that you touched my thing and I touched yours, and I haven't bought it up until now because I was terrified that you'd be disgusted if I told you.

You often tell me about the sex that you have – once a month on average – and you bemoan its scarcity. I tell you about the sex that I've had (five people, ever) and bemoan its scarcity even more vehemently, and then we sit in silence and I'm pretty sure we're thinking the same thing, but nothing's happened, not since the filthy motel in Pottsville. To tell you the truth, I'm a bit scared at the prospect. It's not that I don't want it to, you understand, it's just I'm not sure I could handle you in bed. I'm but a fawn between the sheets; I know not what I do. And you're so experienced.

Once after a big night out you got kicked off a bus for swearing at the driver, and we had to catch a taxi home. The next morning you came over. You went straight into my bedroom when I opened the front door – you didn't even say hi – and jumped into my bed. You had knickers on but no pants, and you didn't remember getting kicked off the bus, but it came back to you when I told the story. We spooned and I had to move my pelvis backwards so that I didn't poke you in the bum. I said to you then that if I had a daughter, I'd name her Molly, but that I'd want to see a picture of what she looked like when she grew up first, because Molly's a great name if you're beautiful (such an innocent name, so provocative if you're pretty) but a terrible name if you're plain. 'Does it suit me?' you asked, and you were smug because you knew the answer. And not wanting to acknowledge the difference in beauty between us, lest you realise that gap and stop getting into bed with me with no pants on, not wanting to inflate your ego, I said that it wasn't your parents fault because they didn't know what you were going to look like, and you should consider changing it. We almost kissed but didn't.

Last February you began to flirt with my father. I've never talked to you about it; I've been too embarrassed to bring it up, but you did. You still do. When I moved back in with him your visits increased significantly, even though I now live further away from you than before. You come over and you wear low-cut tops and short skirts and you chat to him in the kitchen about his work and stroke your hair. You say, 'that's so *interesting*, Martin. You're so *funny*, Martin,' and of course he notices your beautiful legs and bum because he's just a red-blooded male, after all. And I hate knowing that my father and I are imagining fucking the same girl in the same room at the same time. You can appreciate how incestuous that feels, right Molly? It feels like having a threesome: Daddy, you and me, and that's an impression that no son should ever be made to entertain. You told me that you think he's sexy, and yes, I can see that in the fast shrinking pool of middle-aged, middle-class male professionals living on the North Shore, he'd be one of the better catches. He's divorced. He's a college professor. He has broad shoulders and constant stubble and he broke the bridge of his nose playing rugby in the 1980s; a lucky break because it gave him a Roman nose and not a crooked one. Now he has an almost Latin appearance despite his Jewish, Eastern European lineage, the lucky bastard. And I know I'll never look like that, but Molly, have you no shame?

I think it's a passing phase: you've never been with an older man and you think it's a romantic notion. It's literary. It's somehow French. But at the end of the day, Molly, I must inform you that it's me you love, not him. I'm prepared to accept that some of your love for me *resides* in him (just as one who loves a woman very much will love her child too, before they've even met) but that's just a by-product of your love for me, so discard it. Listen, does your forearm hair rise to meet his? Admittedly, I've tried hard to see whether it does, with my heart in my mouth, when we're all in the kitchen and you're standing next to him. But I'm pretty sure it doesn't, Molly. I'm almost certain that it doesn't.

I want you to know that I've talked to my father about it. I had to see how he'd react to my bringing it up, I had to know whether he considered you off limits. It was one of the most uncomfortable things I've ever done. He was making coffee in the kitchen and you had just left the house. I walked into the room and said, casual-as-can-be, 'so what do you think of Molly?' He smiled and looked at me strangely.

'Molly's nice. I like talking to her.' Then silence.

'Why, am I rude to her? I really do like her.'

'No, No,' I said. 'No, I just think she likes you too.' And I scoffed, tried to make it sound trivial.

'I mean, she has a crush on you,' I said. He had his back to me; he was fiddling with the espresso machine.

'Nonsense, Dan, she's just polite.' (Oh, Father, you're just as coy as her.)

'She's ... immature', I said. 'Confident and immature.' I laughed.

'She once said you were good looking, that's all.' When he turned around, with a cup in his hand and an embarrassed smile, I saw that despite my back-peddling I'd confirmed to him what he had long suspected but was too modest (or disbelieving of his good fortune) to admit to himself; his son's beautiful friend wanted to fuck him, and though he tried tactfully to hide it, I could see that he was thrilled at the prospect. But all he said was, 'she's just polite' again and walked quickly out of the room.

Now you know the facts, Molly. And I suppose you're wondering why I'm telling you all of this. The truth is, I have a proposal. Because I know that you love me and you're just confused. And so am I – confused, that is – but I think I know what needs to be done in order to tidy up our situation. Molly, get my father out of your system and then be mine. Sleep with him for one night, exorcise your lust for him, and then you can give your heart to me. Then when we lay in bed together, like the morning after you got kicked off the bus, there'll be nothing to stop us kissing. It can be like that night in Pottsville, but we'll be sober. Because if nothing happens, and the tension continues to grow between you and my father, and parallel to that, the love between us remains – and the hairs on our forearms continue to stretch out towards each other like arms through the bars of a cage – then I really don't know what I'll do. I think I would hurt my father, Molly. Please consider my proposal; it hasn't been easy to write.

Alice

Thomas Gardner

My Alice, my mannerly model of car,
And a model it is, and a means that it is
To get me around and that's why I have called
It my Alice.

What beauty it dons and its body so bronze
Is adored by all those who may view it;
As I ride it each day, in a roundabout way,
They watch me with awe and they marvel and say:
'O, to own such a thing and reap that fair ring
With that key fitting faultlessly into it!'

And, after some time, I came to know how
To care for my coveted car, my creature, my clothing –
Just feed it a little, not too much, not too much,
And a stroke and nice words and to drive it each day,
Yes, a ride every day, for that's what it likes
And performance, conformance will follow.

Alice

One unfortunate day I rode from my office,
Rode Alice to lunch at a cafe,
Where I met a nice lady, mysterious, shady,
A young piece I procured there, presently.
Then I went back to Alice, saw its face full of malice,
As if there was a bee in its bonnet.
I asked what was wrong, but it saw all along
What was happening inside that café.

With a howl and a shriek and hardhearted screech
It fled, although I did entreat and beseech
Her to stay.

I pondered that day, with my car far away,
How fleeting those cars' hearts could be;
After merely a meeting, little more than a greeting,
They left, blaming me for their trickery.
They might sing each to each, but when eating that peach
One discerns the cruel woman's cruel part in it
The ambitions and covetings, prides and disdaining
The slander and mutable flatterings feigning
One imagines the woman's part in it.

So that afternoon, with the time opportune
For the purchase of vehicles aesthetic,
I bought a young car, which is unnamed so far,
But I found her quite cute and cosmetic.

Sophia

Camellia C. Yildirim

I get flashed when I head into the city. Toll collection booths, tourists taking photos as I walk by, the young girls I take back to my room on Thursday nights. I pick them up from their predictably pathetic hospitality jobs and I serve on them. I am a cater waiter for women and I'm as predictable as their minimum wages.

I've got to get back to work, but what are you doing for dinner tonight?

I haven't decided.

How about me?

I might not even be in the city tonight.

Where are you going?

Anywhere. Maybe.

How about here? She points at herself.

I lose myself in their bodies and carve out their chests and sing with their lungs and as I break their hearts they break my faith in hope and humanity and I find myself sinking into their hollowed minds and tar-scarred soles. Women are godly. Empty and limitless. Abandoned and brandished and strong and I breathe lifeless and blink blind and reach for hands that are not there and search for faces that have been left on the pillow covers smudged into the mascara crying down the edge near the bloodied lips. They wait to fall, to jump would mean too much. Without intent or significance. A fear holds them; backing towards the edge, and cumbersome my gaze gnaws at their harrowing sense of reality, hoping to taste those smells and feel those symphonies they bellow as they collapse between me.

Peter asks for another beer and I look at him wearisome and knowing. He doesn't see what's going on with me. I don't know what's going on. He is blind to the bruises and the dimmed light of the bar doesn't help. Hidden behind his own oblivion is mine; I wonder how far I can take this with Peter. The charade we play with each other fulfils the small hopes I have for the regularity of green grass on the other side and the golden seas I have already drowned in. Peter and I weave fractals around the real and around ourselves. We have been lost within the chaos for long enough to forget remembering what is real; we are lost in the edges which do not end and the corners we cannot turn and the resonating perpetuity. Routines end nowhere and we sit with hollow knowledge and nostalgia creeping up on us, itching at the hope that we will remember or that we will see or that we will realise what we have forgotten. The us we used to have and the us we have lost in the belcher chains and chain smoking and smoking jackets. Hollow hope hangs like drip tip leaves and we sit sure with our beers.

I feel the brailed paths as I walk down after dinner with Peter. I wonder how sharp the edges of the grooves are. How would the ground I walk on grate the skin I walk with? The world turns and I walk against the grain and the pink of my skin would colour the blackened path taking me to my bed.

I hit my head and forgot my name the other night. I hit tequila and then I hit my head and I can't remember much more than that. Except for the carpet I forgot my face on. Green, tight pile, polyester. Who the fuck has green carpet in a house? Was it a house? Was it even green? I can't remember why I think it was green.

Sophia, not Coppola, turns to me and rests her hand on my bruised knee. Tom had me down for so long last night but I've been gorging myself on oranges long enough that the bruises don't blue and the blues don't sing low enough. Blue notes ring in my ears and Sophia is looking at me confused and concerned and, from what I can tell, committed.

Her soft curls are running rampant around her face. A face calculus couldn't count. Eyes which turn stars green look at me.

How can I make you happy?

You do.

No, I mean, happy in here. She rests her hand on a cushion of hair and the edges of her mouth curl up and she runs her fingers through my knotted locks which keep safe a reality which exists within me but not without me. And I haven't been there for a while.

Melancholy – *Petra Hanke*

Sunlight and Open Spaces

Agnes Bairstow

It's raining. A grey pall of humidity has settled over the city, the same sick colour as the woollen blankets in the wards. The corridor leading to the operating theatre is cool and there is a smell of rain on asphalt. A window is set into the thick concrete wall at street level, and through it Archie can hear the soft white noise of the rain. He's been in surgery since before lunch and he can still taste the sterile caustic smell of Dettol at the back of his throat.

He closes his eyes and the sound of the raindrops falling sets a meteor shower of bright lights off behind his eyelids. It is an illusion as delicate as a spun glass ornament and it is one that he has no business having.

He loses himself in the bright lights and the smell of the rain. Sometimes the lights are muted, like the faded colour plate from a geography textbook. Today the light is a clean bright white firework spark, like a white phosphorous mortar going off in the night. The clean bright moment of dazzling silence before the fall, except the fall never comes.

There is a brisk sound of leather on lino and Archie opens his eyes. Casually he checks the time on his wristwatch.

– Ah! It's raining. I was going to go for a walk after I had luncheon.

– Yes. At least it's not so hot.

Archie congratulates himself for coming up with this response so quickly. He turns to face the Head Surgeon and looks him in the eye. Dr Johnson nods jovially. He is always serious before surgery and jolly after it. Archie can smell aftershave and carbolic soap.

– Well done closing that surgery, Mr Allan.

– Thank you, sir.

– How would you describe that closure?

– Uneventful, sir.

There is a brief pause. During the War there were always rumours going around that an officer with a strange accent had been seen somewhere, wearing the uniform of a colonel but asking inappropriate and probing questions. There would be something wrong with the way he looked or the way he spoke or the way he lit his cigarette, nothing you could put your finger on. A German spy, a whisper. Archie sometimes fears this is he.

– And if you were called upon to describe it further?

– The skin was brought together with silkworm ligatures which were interrupted to allow for the escape of serum.

– And your opinion on draining the appendix?

– Removal is safer, sir. Remove the source of infection.

– Good lad.

The Head Surgeon gives a satisfied nod and walks away. He is around the age of Archie's father, with greying hair. He is cheerful and donnish, more academic than doctor.

Archie is at the doorway of the resident's tearoom when he sees the Ward Matron come out of the nurse's tearoom. He is hungry and there is a metallic taste in his mouth. He thinks dumbly, automatically: *please, not now.*

– Ah, Mr Allan. I'd like a word, if you're not too busy.

This last is said with the merest gloss of formality: her tone says that she has far more important things to do and doesn't give a damn if it's convenient.

Archie runs over a dry list of tasks in his head: things he has done right today and things she might disapprove of. Forms filled out hurriedly, patients spoken to, a bandage he ordered to be changed.

– Yes, Matron?

The tone of her voice makes a dark, spiky silhouette flash behind his eyelids for a moment: something like the seed pod of a banksia. He's worrying at an old linty button with the fingers of his left hand. He takes his hands out of his pockets and lays them awkward and flat at his sides. She's only half a head shorter than he, wearing flat leather shoes. He can smell the starch coming off her uniform. A momentary sense of injustice strikes him: he can stand here in a suit with frayed cuffs, yet the nurses must wear these preposterous stiff creations.

– The Johnson child. You've given her aspirin.

Archie has so many patients. A child, auburn hair sprayed across the pillow. He can place her now. The dry rasp of her cough as he performed chest auscultations.

– Yes. I'd like to see her temperature coming down soon.

– You prescribed five grains?

Archie realises he is looking at the lino between his feet. He sees himself scrawling the orders. *.5 grains po.* So that's the problem.

– Point five, matron. I prescribed half a grain.

– There are student nurses here, Mr Allan, who are not familiar with the optimal dosage of these medications. They are overenthusiastic.

Kindly prefix your orders with a nought. Your cuffs are frayed.

The matron clacks off and Archie puts his hands back in his pockets. A nought. I ought to care for a nought.

A student doctor from another ward is sitting at the table leafing through the newspaper. Archie doesn't know his name. He goes and pours himself a cup of tea and takes the last sandwich off the tray. Corned beef stained with an exudation of yellow mustard at the corners, and Archie doesn't even flinch.

– Was that her?

– Ward Matron? Yes.

The other doctor grins and folds the newspaper over with a grand rustling sound. Yellow. It is a comforting sound.

– Cor. What'd she get you for?

– Didn't put a nought in front of a decimal.

– Haven't heard that one before.

Archie has seen a seventeen-year-old student nurse burst into tears as soon as the Matron called her name. Everyone but the most senior doctors are afraid of her. You have to have leather skin to not be afraid of her. It is not a proper fear, like the way we fear fire and speed. More wariness mixed with schoolboy shame.

– She never fails to make yer feel as if yer should be ashamed of yerself, does she?

– No. Like a bloody mind-reader.

The tea is strong and black and not too cold and Archie puts his left hand back into his pocket. The other man has two fingers missing off his right hand. The ring and the pinky. Nothing but a patch of smooth scar tissue where they should be.

The *extensor digitorum profundus* bends these fingers toward the palm and helps us grip. Can he hold a scalpel? Archie is careful to look away.

Did he leave these fingers in the mud of another country? He curls the fingers of his left hand toward the palm. Feels the nails there.

Archie finishes his tea. He feels as if he should say something else but the other man has returned to his paper, so he puts on his hat and leaves.

Outside, the air is cool. There is the fresh smell of the rain, and a stronger smell of kerosene and coal. Archie wants to walk. He wants to be tired. Just as he starts to cross the street he hears someone call his name. He realises too late that it is Stuart, rushing up to the side entrance with a sheaf of papers rustling under one arm. He wonders what Stuart is doing and what the papers are for and dimly realises that he does not care. He might have been asked to help out with a lecture or a tutorial, and now there is just a feeling of being released from obligations that he is expected to happily volunteer for.

A woman in the park calls for her children, and Archie can hear them laughing. He can't stop thinking of a hand with two missing fingers. The thought grates and sticks like the sound of a bone saw and he takes out a cigarette and lights it to stop it from continuing. This technique works, and he walks on in the cool afternoon.

Two men in overalls eating sandwiches made from thick white bread, their fingernails black around the edges with grease. The thick grey smell of a cigar. The grass. He tries not to think of the hospital and instead rolls a textbook diagram of the human hand across his mind's eye. *The wrist joint is comprised for the most part of the articulation of the distal articular surface of the radius with the scaphoid and the lunate.* He learned the bones by rote at university, and he can recall them now easily. It gives him an obscure satisfaction to do so. There is a vaguely rotting smell of wet grass and a richer brown smell of earth.

There is a man standing on a soapbox somewhere near the centre of the park. Archie can hear the high murmur of his voice when he's still a hundred yards off. There is a small crowd of people gathered around, loafers mostly, with a few who look to be on their lunch breaks.

– DISEASE is rampant in this city! Everywhere I look around me I see FILTH! And DEGRADATION.

It is an anaemic-looking man with wet eyes behind thick wire-framed glasses. A natty little brown suit and a little black hat. He is a showman. He punctuates his address by waving a thick sheaf of papers, sometimes slashing the air in front of his torso, sometimes whacking them against his leg. He goes on about SLUMS and SMOKE and CONSUMPTION and ROT and DRUNKENNESS and his rich tenor voice, raised above the crowd, gives to Archie a flash of wine-red at every emphasised word, like an advertising hoarding seen from a bus.

– What is the solution to all this? SUNSHINE. Sunshine and open spaces! Give the children fresh air and expose them to the fortifying rays of sunlight! Buy my pamphlet on ray therapy!

Most of the crowd turns away murmuring, but a tired-looking woman in a drab woollen dress steps forward and presses a tuppenny piece into the spruiker's hand. A fat pink man in a bowler hat does the same. *Sunlight won't do much for your gout, mate*, Archie thinks. The man and the woman walk off in different directions with their tracts in hand. One of the children laughs somewhere off to one side, a thin clear sound. Archie coughs. The man straightens pamphlets and sets them in a neat little pile on his wooden crate. Archie thinks of sunlight. He wants to talk to the man but at the same time a small leaden weight of fear has settled itself in his gut. He is afraid of normal things, like loud noises and the sudden shadowy rustling of a man standing up next to him on the tram. This is an abnormal reaction.

– Yer a medical man I see.

His stethoscope, still strung around his neck. Three pounds from the medical supplier's shop in the city, engraved carefully with his initials.

All the way to France and back and here it is, strung around his neck not in his briefcase like it should be. Archie takes his stethoscope and puts it into his blazer pocket.

– Yes.

– I'm somewhat inclined in that way meself. Not a professional, you see, but a skilled amateur, you could say.

He talks like that, all verbal flourishes. Performing to an audience of one.

– Yer a doctor?

– Yes, over at the hospital.

– How'd yer find it over there?

Archie doesn't know quite what to say. The man stares at him expectantly.

– It's crowded.

That isn't quite what he meant what to say, but it's true. The smell of cologne lingering with sweat as someone pushes past him on the stairs. The hailstone sound of the feet going back and forth, back and forth, and the patients, the coughing, squirming wretched mass of them. Archie can feel the closeness of them there, on his skin. He does not like to be close to too many people any more. Sometimes it is all he can do not to scream. Release a giant orange cloud of his anguish. Archie swallows hard. His throat hurts.

– This whole city's crowded mate. You see all them slums down there? Teeming with poisonous emanations.

He seems to savour the last word. Emanations. Ensure that the sick room is well ventilated to allow for the escape of sickly emanations. It seems like too old a word. Older than this age and the smoky, bustling filthiness of it. Archie swallows hard again and sees the other man look him up and down.

– Listen, are you orright?

– Yes, of course.

But none of the usual excuses come: heatstroke, fatigue, a chill. He can feel the buildings pressing down on him. The cars and trains and rushing feet, all roaring outside the fragile oasis of the park. Archie puts his left hand into his trouser pocket and closes it tight around the handful of change he has in there. It's warm. He feels as if he might very slowly be falling apart. He takes in the other man's concerned glance and speaks again.

– I think I agree with you. Everything here is too close. If I could I think I'd get away.

He looks up into the man's wet brown eyes. His wire-rimmed spectacles are thick and one lens is smeared slightly with moisture, fogged from the rain. The other man thrusts a handful of paper at him.

– Take this. With my compliments.

It's a couple of pamphlets. The top one says 'An INTRODUCTION to a SYSTEM for regaining Strength and Vigour'.

Archie reaches into his pocket for a halfpenny piece but the other man reaches out and closes his hand around his wrist. Archie jerks back. He can't help it.

– No. Don't pay me.

He lowers his voice and speaks out of the side of his sad, moustachioed mouth.

– It's guff, mostly, but it's nothing that people don't need to hear. Sunshine and clean air, that's what we need.

Archie folds the paper into his blazer pocket.

– Thanks.

– No worries.

The little man has already turned away to his piles of paper and his wooden box. Archie puts his hands into his pockets and turns away down the path. When he gets to the street he decides to cross and walk in the direction of the Botanic Gardens. The sun is coming out and he can feel a patch of sweat building at the small of his back. When he gets to the sandstone gates of the Gardens and walks into the shade of the trees it is cooler. There, on the sculpted paths, it is quieter as well. Archie clears his throat and drinks deeply from an ornate drinking fountain. The water has a tinny taste like stagnant tank water but it is refreshing. He reads the plaque at the foot of it as he wipes his mouth with the back of his hand: it is a donation from the Freemasons. He reads the plaque at the base of a normal-looking clump of grass. It is some sort of exotic species. What makes the gardeners want to plant these things?

Archie indulges in a fantasy of being a gardener; not the grubby sort that trims grass or hedges, but the sort who stubbornly raises these plants from foreign places, cataloguing and trimming them. Archie has a school friend who is studying agriculture at the university. He talks with great zeal about grain and soil improvement and irrigation. Going out into the great dusty waste out there and saying, *I will stay here, I will try to grow things.*

Up ahead of him on the path there is a couple: a well-built young man with his arm around a girl wearing a plain shift and a hat. Archie does not want to disturb them, so he turns down the other path. After a while he sits down under a tree on a patch of grass, and reads the pamphlet. The man was right, there isn't much to it. Sunshine and open spaces. Clean air and clean water, a cold water bath every morning. There's a little chit at the back you can snip out to send away for more pamphlets or patent medicines.

Archie starts walking diagonally across a large expanse of grass. There is a dull pain at the back of his throat, so he swallows then scrubs his hands across his face, hard. His hands still smell tarry, like carbolic soap. At the far end of the gardens is Mrs Macquarie's chair, the bench convicts carved from stone for the Governor's wife. Wet blades of grass gather on the toes of Archie's shoes.

The sun is shining fully now and the wide dome of the sky overhead meets the grass and this part of the world is very silent. An Indian myna chitters nearby, the noise a deep blue staccato. Archie is halfway across the grass when the pain in his throat condenses into a huge lump, a physical thing, and escapes as a deep gasping sob. He stands in the middle of the grass and puts his hands to his face and cries. He wishes to sink to the grass and do nothing, let the rain and heat beat at him until he is nothing and no-one. He squats down on his haunches and stares into the sky.

He puts his legs out in front of him and lies back with his arm over his eyes. He lies like that for a long time, until his thoughts have turned to more mundane things, like the water that has soaked into the seat of his trousers. He gets up and brushes himself off. He goes back to the water fountain and washes his face off and feels a little bit better. Then he walks home. It takes him two hours and he has only done it once before, when he was roaring drunk and less aware of things like blisters and heat. When he gets there his landlady offers him tea and he takes it without looking her in the eye. He is so footsore and tired that he falls asleep in his shirtsleeves and underwear. He jolts awake at four am, disoriented and thirsty. He lies there thinking of open spaces and sunlight, yet when he looks in his blazer pockets he finds nothing but his stethoscope and an old linty button. The pamphlet is not there.

I'll go to the country, he thinks, and it's the shakiest kind of start.

Hunting and Gathering

Rosemary Vickers

This Easter I'm looking for mushrooms,
but they don't seem to be in the same places as they were
last year, or the year before.

The grass is too long and too lush between the tussocks
and cowpats around the dam.
Lots of puffballs, and yellow fungus and small
toadstools, but no mushrooms; although it has rained and
now it is almost sunny.

Perhaps it's too cold? There must be some precise,
mystical permutation which clicks open a
secret spring in the mushroom spores –
and up pop mushrooms!

Meanwhile I'm walking slowly, ruminating,
and wandering and looking,
with eyes searching and sweeping over whitened bone
fragments, quartzy rocks, dead pale leaves,
watching the black cockatoos flying backwards and
forwards.

Suddenly there's a mushroom and then another.
But not in the same place as last year or the year
before.

You'd have to know the country very well
and walk it season after season round and about,
following the same slope of the hill, feeling with skin
and feet how wet the grass, how warm the air, how boggy or
dry. To know each patch of trees, which place, which year,
which kind of fungi.

I've only known this particular piece of bushy farm for
about five years.

You'd need to know it for twenty years (or a lifetime or many
lifetimes) to confidently, easily find
what I now find by chance – half a dozen mushrooms
which grow in that part of the ground just beneath
a big tree where the sheep rest.
Enough to make a salad more interesting.
But not quite enough to feed a child or a
tribe.

So I walk, as other women have walked, stringing out
across a grassy hillside. Easy to walk so
with child on back or hip, carrying and wandering,
picking and searching, pausing to
watch the flight of birds.

The Echo

Joshua Mostafa

The Echo stood on a corner halfway up Seven Sisters Road; it *still* stood,
that April afternoon under a thickening sky, its dilapidated sign swinging
in the wind with a weary defiance. It was an old pub, its brickwork
marinated in secrets and history. During the Blitz, buildings on both
sides had been erased in a single night, earning the Echo a reputation
for providence. A week later, a bomb had dropped out of the evening
sky without warning, bursting through tile and plaster into a crowded
bar, snuffing out the lives of half the revellers and the entire band, but
leaving the facade it showed to the street intact. For nearly two decades
it remained a hollow presence, under threat of demolition. New owners
renovated it in the sixties without any attempt at reconciling its sombre
masonry with the gaudy psychedelic aesthetics of its new interior. The
Zombies were billed for the reopening, their first gig since a tour of the
USA. The queue went around the corner, and anxious to make a splash,
the owners let in too many. The air was stifling, the drinks overpriced, and
the crowd, pressed between window frame and wainscoting, began to get

restive. When the band faltered through a rendition of 'She's Not There' marred by feedback screeching from the PA, people began to demand their money back. Fights broke out, windows were smashed, and the law had to be called in. More dud gigs followed that inauspicious beginning, despite the best efforts to ventilate the venue and improve the sound system; every band that played there complained of something that spoilt their performance: bad acid, bad luck, bad vibes. It was that last, most damning slur that denied it the iconic rock-and-roll status its owners had been so determined to give it, and pushed it back into obscurity.

And yet the Echo had persisted. The city around it had changed, boarding over the shop windows of once-bustling high streets in the seventies; or, conversely, in the following decades, carving new strips of gentrification through the proletarian heartlands. The Echo was the borough's fulcrum of continuity, not unchanging, but sedimenting layers of time one on top of another. The Echo survived the enthusiasm of the eighties and nineties for refashioning old pubs into smart bars. It remained a music venue, of a more modest kind; the Echo's resident trad jazz band, the Alley Cats, pulled in a decent crowd most weekends.

On that particular Friday, the weathered face of the Echo, nestled between a kebab shop and a service station on one side, and an upmarket beauty salon on the other, was being observed from the balcony of a hostel on the other side of the junction. Its dingy windows and graffiti-streaked walls made it an unlikely object of the great and growing hope being invested in it by its observer, James, a young man seated in a fraying armchair, one leg hoisted over its arm. Between glances at the old pub, he was restoring the sheen to every inch of a trumpet of almost equal age. A flier beside him announced 'Live Jazz at the Echo with Sofia Trieste and the Alley Cats'. It was almost time for his audition; the band had recently lost their trumpet player, whose head among the faces of the band on the flier was obscured by a bulbous glass ashtray. James fancied that beneath the translucent facets of the ashtray it was his own face, cheeks puffed, among the Alley Cats. He shifted his weight in the armchair; the passport curling in his back pocket was becoming uncomfortable to sit on. There were two weeks left on his visa waiver. The prospect of home, hot and dusty, did not appeal.

James ran a fingertip along the trumpet's brass surface, inspecting the sheen, and his own reflection in it, elongated and corrugated by the dents of many years. His new trilby had made a hole in his dwindling funds, and he could not be sure if it was the fault of the distorted reflection, but it seemed to be too big for his head. But he was too badly in need of a haircut to go without it. James settled the trumpet in its case, and took it downstairs. He did not want to be late.

As he stepped out of the hostel's front door, a reedy voice hailed him. 'Here's Dizzy Gillespie now! Today's the big day, right?'

James turned, unwilling. He did not feel like speaking to Milosz, not at that moment, though he also felt that he should be grateful. If it were not for Milosz, he would never have got the audition, or even known they were looking for a trumpet player. But he had no time now for Milosz, his nervous laugh, or the bottle of lager he was proffering. 'Yeah, but no thanks. I'm just about to head over there. Thanks for hooking me up with this, by the way. I owe you big.'

Milosz clapped his shoulder. They had both been at the hostel, and in London, for six weeks – a long time, in hostel terms – but while James was still bewildered by the size and the density of London, Milosz had settled in immediately. He'd made contacts everywhere: artists, promoters, coke dealers, and, crucially, the manager of the Alley Cats. 'All good, anything for a buddy. You want a little line before you go? Pep you up a bit? No? What, you don't think *she*'ll approve?'

'Who?'

'The voice of Jimmy heaven. Sofia ... what is it, Testy, Titty? If you get this gig ...' Milosz's lopsided grin straightened into a long face, Oriental-caricature. 'A wise man say. He who screw with crew, end up in deep shit.'

The Saturday before, James and Milosz had gone to the Echo to see the Alley Cats. Afterwards, crossing the road back to the hostel, James had wondered out loud why Sofia Trieste, the singer, was wasting her talents in the poky little pub. He had wondered out loud, and at length, why she had never released a record. 'I've looked on the net and there's no mention of her doing anything except these little gigs at the Echo. You've heard her, she could get signed in a second.' Milosz had slurred something about it being who you knew, not what. Sleep with the right people and the doors would open. James' response, a passionate diatribe on behalf of talent and against society, had been louder than it needed to be. It was sharpened by his sense that Milosz had no right to talk, since he had no talent of his own. They had arrived in the hallway at the hostel by that point, and the warden had told him to put a sock in it. Today, disengaging himself from Milosz and his jibes, James' irritation was tempered by the thought that Milosz had a talent after all, a talent for collecting the right people. It was thanks to this that James would have a chance to prove his own.

The first few drops of rain had begun to fall when James crossed the street. The pub was closed, but there was a door around the side held ajar with a brick. A fat and dishevelled man of about fifty leant against the doorframe, a cigarette smoking in the corner of his mouth. Thinking he might be a tramp about to ask him for change, James avoided his eye, but as he neared the door, he recognised the man as the Alley Cats' drummer.

James stuck out his hand. 'Hi, I'm James. How are you going? I'm here for the audition. Great set you guys played last week.'

The shabby man raised his eyes slowly and his face broke into an amiable smile, creased with habit. 'Sergey,' he said.

They shook hands. James tried to think of something to say that would make him sound like a professional, not a fan.

Sergey offered him a cigarette. James didn't smoke, but he accepted it anyway. He tried to inhale casually and without coughing. The silence seemed more natural now they were both smoking.

'So. You play trumpet?' Sergey indicated the battered vinyl case in James' hands.

James had an impulse to confide in him, to tell him that he had loved the sound of the trumpet since a humid December day in Rangewood, eight years old, cooling his back on smooth metal where the sofa fabric had frayed, waiting for his turn at the video game, when he heard a melody drift in from the kitchen radio, full of melancholy swagger; that this melody had stayed with him ever since; that the electric guitar was a faceless, clumsy thug, the flute a sissy, the saxophone a cheap floozy; that only the trumpet was noble, deep-souled, brave and true. Instead he said: 'Yeah. I've always … that's what I play.'

'I have been playing drums for a long time. A long time but only here. Only in this place.' Sergey's eyes, grey and sunken beneath the folds of his face, were sad. 'You start to play with us, you might find you are a bit stuck. Are you sure you want to play with us?'

'You guys are exactly the kind of band I want to be in.'

'You better come on in then.' Sergey spat the cigarette butt onto the pavement, and led James into the Echo. Not to the stage in the main bar, but to a large and dilapidated room with the windows bricked up and variegated with mould.

The band was playing 'Solitude', in a loose, casual way, sitting on chairs facing each other. There was Sofia, perched on a bar stool off to one side, writing in a spiral-bound book and paying no attention to the others. James tried not to stare. She seemed entirely unlike her glamorous stage persona: middle-aged, hunched over, straggly haired, a pair of John Lennon glasses resting on her long nose. He felt suddenly very young.

'The trumpet player is here,' Sergey announced to the room, making his unhurried way to the kit and starting to drum as if he had been there the whole time.

Sofia got up from her seat and walked towards him. He shook her hand, trying for a firm grip, and wondered as she pulled hers back if he had squeezed her fingers too tightly. She looked him up and down with black eyes. He wished he had worn something smarter than his tatty sheepskin coat. 'We're a bit stuck at the moment, you know. Our trumpet player was really good, but he couldn't keep it together. In rehab now. Are you reliable?'

'Totally, a hundred percent,' said James, and immediately wished he had thought of some cooler, less eager way of replying.

'You're Australian, are you? You legal to work here?'

'Yes,' he lied. He would have to get a work visa. Would he need to leave the country to do it? Could he just overstay?

'We'll have to throw you in at the deep end. There's a gig here tomorrow night. We can't audition you properly, but just join in now while we run through everything. You should be fine, we're just playing standards.'

'Like we play other songs!' said Sergey. Sofia ignored him.

Sweat made James' fingers slippery on the stops of his trumpet. His throat was dry from the cigarette he'd smoked outside and he felt the wool of his jacket prickle the skin around the back of his neck. Repressing the urge to cough made his eyes water.

He forced himself to relax as they played the first song, and ignore that he was playing in the same band as the woman with the most beautiful voice he had ever heard. He was taken aback when the piano player announced the next, 'Cottontail'; he had never played it before, nor laid eyes on the score. He decided to confine himself to the most elementary phrase of the trumpet part, riff around that a little, and hope that they would interpret that as styling rather than ineptitude.

As the song struck up, though, he found the notes with ease, as if he had played it a hundred times before. He even managed a creditable solo. Meeting the eyes of the piano player as they came to the bridge, he hoped for some acknowledgement, but he was playing with his eyes half-closed, and when he nodded, James could not be sure if it was a sign of approval, or just nodding to the beat.

James knew he was playing at his best. A deftness of touch beyond his usual ability was animating his fingers and his lips; it was as if the songs were playing themselves through him. But there was no response, either good or bad, from the band. Perhaps they were too cool to show enthusiasm.

At the end of the set, exhausted, he had no idea if they had been impressed, or not. He had managed to lose himself for a while and enjoy playing with a band, every one of whom, he was sure, had been playing for at least as long as he'd been alive, and to whom the songs seemed as natural as a conversation between good friends.

No-one paid him much attention, which he hoped was a good sign. At the same time, he was sure it was a bad one. They were all polite, but that itself excluded him from their light, gently mocking banter with each other. He imagined they had all known each other for years. He did not dare ask if, having heard him play, they still wanted him at the gig the next night. He put his trumpet back in its case and started to put his coat on.

'Aren't you staying for a drink?' It was Sofia, suddenly beside him, her hand on his arm. 'We usually have a couple after the rehearsal before the doors open.'

Surely she would not ask him to stay if he had done badly. He followed her through to the main bar, relieved and a little giddy.

The decor of the Echo had been accreted continuously since its restoration; the debris of the past had never been cleared away. Old posters for gigs crowded the walls. There were flyers for gigs from the late eighties, not framed as artefacts but just still hanging around from the time of the gigs, yellowed and peeling. The tatty upholstery had been installed no more recently than the seventies. The manager, shouting at the bar staff as they put out the chairs, a half cigar jammed between his gums in defiance of law and the pub's own rules, could have been a product of any time in the past century, or conceivably the one before. James and Sofia sat by a window underneath an old 'Vertigo' poster. The rain was lashing down.

'Look at it. Nothing like where you're from. Where did you say, again?'

'Queensland.'

'That's in the north, isn't it? I can't say I imagined much of a jazz scene there.'

James grinned. 'Tell me about it. That's why I'm here.'

'It's a long way. You could have gone to New York. That's closer, isn't it? I'd go there if I had the chance.'

'My aunt and uncle live in Birmingham. I stayed with them for a while when I came out. And to be honest I was just ready to get out of Rangewood, wherever I was going.'

'You make it sound so bad!'

Gin and tonic loosened his tongue. He told her about his home town, its insularity, and how he'd longed to escape; about the band he'd joined at high school, a funk outfit and the only alternative to rock music, and its debut at the end-of-year battle of the bands. As they floundered under the indifferent gaze of the crowd, the guitarist had tried to rescue the performance with a Guns N' Roses style solo that had nothing to do with 'Papa's Got a Brand New Bag'. To James' horror the crowd had loved it.

She threw her head back and laughed. 'I see why you had to leave. I have the opposite problem. I grew up on jazz. My father was a musician, and so was my granddad. Can't escape it, you could say.' She smiled an odd smile. It didn't make her look happy in the slightest.

'Runs in the family, then. You've got an incredible voice.'

'Thank you.'

'I mean, it's like nothing I've heard before. You're wasted in this place, you know, this little pub. You could go anywhere, do anything!'

'Maybe I'm too set in my ways,' she said lightly, then indicated the bar. 'Look, now they've opened the pub all the suits are coming in. Let's get out of here. It's coming up to tea time. Do you have plans?'

'Not really,' he said slowly, wondering how he should proceed. Was she interested in him? If so, he didn't know how he felt. In successive Saturday nights at the Echo, cramped in amongst the crowd that always packed out the pub, James had fallen in love with her voice. Now, face to face with its owner, he could not shake the feeling that he was being chatted up by a friend of his mother. 'Do you know somewhere good?'

Outside, the rain was coming down in waves, filling the gutters and scoring the road surface. A dog ran by, fur plastered to its sides like a giant rat. James wrestled with his umbrella, almost dropping his trumpet case. The wind twisted the spokes of the umbrella and inverted it, flapping it about like a misshapen flag.

Sofia hailed a cab. With the trumpet case beside him they were close together in the back seat. 'Where are we going?'

'My place.' She looked up at him, mock-repressive. 'Don't get the wrong idea now, mister. I'm just thinking with you staying in a hostel, and I know I'm broke, probably neither of us can afford to get the bill if we eat out. I made some pesto this afternoon.' James smiled but didn't reply. He could not quite put Milosz' cynical line – sleeping with people to open doors – out of his mind.

Sofia's flat was a tiny studio with a lot crammed into it. There were paintings stacked behind the sofa, and the coffee table was just a sheet of glass on a big stack of books. The wall adjoining the hearth had floor-to-ceiling shelves, full of LPs, and there was an overflow of CDs and records piled up in front of them.

'Sit down if you can find somewhere. This is me, I'm afraid.' Sofia went through to the kitchen.

There was nowhere to sit, so James stood by the bay window. There was a cage half-hidden by the curtains and he pulled them back to look at the elaborate curved bars. The cage rested at a slight angle, as if it rested on a slope. The door was missing and the hinges twisted outward. There was no sign of any creature, but a bar across the centre suggested it was a birdcage. There was something protruding from underneath it, the corner of a spiral-bound book, which was upsetting its balance. James pulled it out. It looked similar to the one Sofia had been writing in when he had first entered the bar. He wondered if he should open it or put it back.

'Red or white?' Sofia called from the kitchen.

'Up to you.' James opened the notebook at random. Every inch of it was covered: old newspaper cuttings and sepia photographs had been pasted in, and a scrawl, indifferent to rules or margins and decorated with swirling curlicues and flourishes, filled up the rest of the space.

… her fiancé was in North Africa at the time, there was no way of getting news, he must have found out when he got back. I don't remember him,

but I remember remembering him. When I'm in there, I know him as well as I know myself, but it's completely one-way – she doesn't know anything I know. She's worried about him, even though he was perfectly fine. Still lived around the corner 'til a few years ago – found his obit in a back issue of the Gazette. I might have run into him without knowing – on the bus, or at Tesco's. How strange it would have been to see him, out here, as he had become ...

A microwave door closed and glasses clinked. James flipped the page to read a little more. A picture, photocopied from a printed book, had been stapled in. It was an old-fashioned handbill for a jazz concert. The band were all dressed up smartly, and young, especially the trumpet player, a red-haired boy of about eighteen, or perhaps younger. The centre of attention was a brunette with strikingly large eyes and a hairdo with layered curls. A caption beneath it read: 'Daisy Miller and the Hackney All-Stars in a special performance at the Echo'.

He set the book down quickly on the couch as Sofia came back in with two glasses. 'I went with the red. It's not too bad. Shove those books off the couch there, will you.'

James stacked the books against the wall, a small and futile gesture of order in the middle of the chaos. 'You have so many records and CDs. I thought I had a good collection.'

'It's easier when people give them to you.' Sofia sat down next to him in the space he'd cleared and passed him a glass. 'The only effort is sorting through the stuff they give me and throwing out the rubbish.'

'Any of them by you?'

'No.'

'Have you not recorded anything?'

'Not for a long time. I did some recording about ten years ago, just a couple of demos.'

'I was saying to my mate the other day, it's just wrong you haven't got a record deal. I know because I looked you up online, couldn't find anything. It doesn't make sense!'

She smiled. 'My demo must have been crap, then.'

'Was that with the Alley Cats?'

'I was with a different band then. We didn't have a name; we hadn't got that far yet.' Her eyes unfocused. 'Mind you, the Alley Cats are always changing. They may as well be a different band now. Our old trumpet player is only the most recent one to lose the plot. I'm the only constant, I think, over the years.'

'What about the manager? He must have been there a while.'

'Yeah, he's as much of a part of the pub as the dry rot.'

'I can imagine he's been there since Daisy Miller played there!'

Sofia was suddenly intent on him. Her voice was still light, but also cold, suspicious. 'How do you know about Daisy Miller?'

James shifted on the couch, suddenly uncomfortable. Sofia noticed the notebook beside him. She dropped her glass and grabbed the book. Burgundy stained the carpet. 'How much have you read?' she demanded, a rush of blood rising in her cheeks.

'Just a page or two ... I probably shouldn't have ...'

'No! No you shouldn't have! I think if I invite someone into my house I expect them not to pry and to spy within five minutes ...' She cut off, visibly getting control of herself. 'You'd better go. I'll see you tomorrow at the gig.'

'I'm really sorry, I just ...'

'Go.'

It was possible, if you knew the nature of the Echo's walls, and had enough patience, to hear old sounds return, and catch glimpses of past scenes stitched like patchwork scraps onto the present. After the glasses were cleared away and the tabletops wiped; after the jukebox, playing its hurry-up-and-go-home selection of thrash metal, country and Celine Dion, had wound down; after the lights were dimmed, the door closed and the footsteps of the last member of staff had faded away; there, in the gloom, the walls of the pub began to resonate.

The vibrations of night after night jazz, blues, laughter, after-work drinks, the crashing of glasses dropped from drunk or clumsy fingers, the ribald comments of red-faced men with thick fingers wrapped around their pints of dark, flecked ale. Every belch, every shouted argument, every phrase of the tenor sax had been absorbed into the old walls, along with the years of cigarette smoke and the tang of old beer. There was no order to how they emerged. A giggle and a whisper from the mid-seventies would be followed by a sour diatribe about the boss. If you were lucky you could hear whole songs, perhaps even entire sets from the early forties, or the chirruping of the birds that had been the pub's only inhabitants during its derelict years.

If there was a pattern to the times the old sounds resurfaced, it was when the pub was at its noisiest and busiest: a clarinet solo from one of the last gigs before the bomb fell on the Echo, harmonising with the present-day band playing the same song. Or at the quietest times, after a long period of silence. Perhaps two hours, a long two hours if you had stayed back to hear it, knowing you had to stay completely silent. Make the slightest sound yourself in one of those moments, and the sounds would stop. An easy two hours if you had played a gig to a packed house, tried to follow the singer out afterwards when she left without a word, failed to find her, returned to drink round after round of shots in a lock-in with the drummer and the bassist, rested your head for a moment in your hands to stop it spinning, then awoke two hours later, head on the table in the corner of the bar.

James didn't open his eyes, but he could tell the lights were out. There was pain, and there was thirst. Dizziness, nausea, drifting sounds of music. If he moved he would split, or at least vomit. Breath had to be regulated with a sip of air, carefully exhaled. To gulp would be foolhardy. What was that music? Surely everyone had gone home.

His head was pounding. He wasn't sure if he was really awake or if he was hearing the soundtrack from his dreams. The sound kept changing, snippets of this and that, as if an inexpert disc jockey was randomly flicking the crossfader. Then a melody came through, strong, and a voice, rising through a buzz of many voices. It was Sofia's voice, unmistakably, and wasn't that his own trumpet line? There, that difficult key change he had been worried about, but had pulled off perfectly. Someone must have recorded the gig, he thought. The strange thing was that it did not sound like a recording. It was as if the band were playing in the room with him.

The song finished, and applause rose to a deafening level. James sat up, unsteady, and his chair scraped loudly against the floor. Instantly the sound stopped, and it was silent and dark except for the glow of a cigarette across the room.

'Sergey,' said James, holding the side of his head that hurt worse. 'What time is it?'

'You aren't much of a drinker,' said Sergey with a deep laugh, leaning against the bar and pouring out the last of a bottle into two glasses. 'A few nights, though, you can build up a tolerance.'

'Did you hear that? Where was that music coming from? That was from tonight, right?'

'It's so hard to tell now. We play the same songs over and over, and I've been here for many years, you know. So many years.' He walked over and set down one of the glasses in front of James.

'No thanks, I'd be sick. It was definitely tonight, I remember playing that bit.'

'You're not listening to me. We play the *same* songs. Not a little bit different, the same. Us, the ones before us, the ones who will come after us. The same, every time.' He sighed. 'It's hard for some. It doesn't bother me. For a drummer, you see, it's good to be perfect, to be consistent. I wasn't much of a drummer before I came here. That last trumpet player, he could have gone places. It drove him mad. It's bad for people like him. Sofia too. People with real talent. She hates it here. It's a shame, you know.'

James forced his eyes to focus on what he could see of Sergey in the glow of his cigarette. He seemed to be serious about what he was saying, but it did not make sense. A rush of nausea passed through his body, and a sharp taste rose to the back of his tongue. He made it to the bathroom, but there was no time to get into the cubicle. He covered the basin in thin, foamy puke. Some of it splashed up onto the mirror.

He wound a few squares of paper roll around his hand, and wiped the mirror's surface. The face that became visible was unlike his own: pale, freckled, ginger-haired, a teenage boy's face. He blinked at it, and the boy blinked back. He cupped two hands and splashed himself, drawing the water up and over his head. When his eyes were clear of water, it was own face looking back at him, bleary and dishevelled.

James stumbled out of the bathroom. 'Fucking hell, Sergey, what were we drinking? Did we have absinthe? I think I just hallucinated. I looked in the mirror and I saw a face.'

Sergey nodded with interest, but without surprise. 'What did it look like?'

'A boy. I think, out of a picture I saw at Sofia's house.'

'Yes, that's right. Jonny something. We all have one.'

'Have one what?' James had begun to feel afraid for his own mental wellbeing. Perhaps it was not the drink. It had started earlier in the evening, before they had started on the vodka and schnapps. Memories of the gig itself began to piece themselves together in his mind. He had been concentrating too hard on following the songs to pay much attention to the audience, but he distinctly recalled a series of flashes when his vision had split entirely in two, one eye seeing the room as it was, the other some other room, like yet unlike, superimposed, one lit brighter than the other, two different crowds occupying the same space. A man in a hoodie and jeans had overlapped with another with a waistcoat and slicked-down hair.

Then the other room had vanished, as quickly as it had appeared. But later on in the gig he had turned towards Sofia, and for a moment he thought he saw the face of Daisy Miller, the girl from the photocopied handbill. Then her hair had fallen forward across her face; when she brushed it back, it had been Sofia, after all. He feared that a madness, an obsession of some kind, was engulfing him. If so, it had come out of nowhere. He had never known anything like it before. To try to clear his mind he returned to what Sergey had been saying. 'What did you mean about Sofia? If she hates it, why does she play here?'

Sergey smiled sadly. 'She can leave, we can all leave, but it does no good. Maybe for you it's not too late. Try it, when you get home. Try to play a little tune. Anything. You'll see what I mean. If you want to make something of yourself outside this pub, and you find you can still hold a tune, then go, and don't come back here ever again. Otherwise,' he chuckled again, 'I'll see you back here next week. And the week after that ...'

James checked the time on his phone. Half past three. If Sergey had been there the whole time, still drinking spirits, he must have long since passed the point of making sense. 'I'd better go home. Let's talk about this another time though, yeah?' He gathered up his coat and trumpet case.

Sergey made a motion that could have been a nod, could have been a shrug, and blew a smoke ring that twisted and fell apart as it crossed into a thin spike of light from the window.

James was not sure whether to be elated or terrified. The trip had been more than he had hoped for. He was in a great band, playing every weekend to a lively crowd. Within the walls of the pub, he could play the trumpet with a flair far beyond his own natural ability. If, a week previously, someone had showed him how he could now play the trumpet, and asked him what he would give for it, James supposed he would have set no limit.

But the price was heavy. It did not feel as if he himself was playing the trumpet. The day after that first gig, James remembered Sergey's words, and tried playing something simple: 'Basin Street Blues'. His fingers were slow and clumsy, and his lips felt numb, as if anaesthetised. When he reached for the notes in his mind, he came up empty.

He put it down to the hangover, although a cold and shapeless fear settled over him and would not shift. The following night, unable to settle, he got out of bed, picked up his trumpet and made his way down to the Echo. Last orders had been called, but the doorman recognised him and let him in. He rushed down the stairs to the little rehearsal room, lifted the trumpet to his lips: fluid, effortless, beautiful melody. At the same time, another's thoughts crowded his mind; he felt the presence of the boy Sergey had mentioned, Jonny. All his senses suddenly engaged, as if his own life was a dream from which he was awakening. Lowering the trumpet, he would be left on his own again, filling his own shoes.

He wanted desperately to speak to the rest of the band, but he had no-one's phone number. He wondered if like him, they each shared those moments on the stage with some unknown other. Thinking back, there had been a complicity between them, something in their glances, the way they chatted about everything except the band, the pub, or the music. He wished he had paid more attention to the surroundings when he had gone to Sofia's flat; he had no idea now how to get back there. The change from Sofia's speaking voice, thin and high-pitched, to the rich contralto when she sang, made a kind of sense, inasmuch as any of it made sense. It was not Sofia who was singing, but Daisy Miller, just as it was not James who could riff so easily on songs he had never played before, but Jonny, whose freckled face, reflected in the curve of his trumpet, filled James with a desire to strike him, if it were possible to hit a phantom, one that seemed to share the same physical space that James himself occupied.

James was also beginning to hate trad jazz. Back at the hostel he would put his headphones on and listen to Miles Davis, and wish he could play something in that vein. Or play anything, inside the Echo or out, except the Alley Cats' repertoire of a few dozen standards. He did not know if he could live like this, as the others did, playing every week in a small pub until he had no more breath to blow down the trumpet.

On the day of their next gig, James sat and waited in the main bar. Sofia arrived ten minutes before they were about to go on; she avoided his eye as she crossed the floor towards the back, but he followed her through to the corridor leading to the rehearsal room. 'Sofia!'

She turned, showing reluctance, her mouth set in a hard line.

'I can't play anything, anymore. Except when I come here. It's been driving me crazy all week. What's happening to me? Is it like that for you?'

Her eyes softened behind her owlish spectacles. 'I'm sorry. Yes. It's the same for all of us.'

'Half the time, when I'm here – I don't know how to say it. I'm me but I'm also someone else. Like you and Daisy Miller. It's freaking me out. I don't believe in … that kind of stuff.'

'It's not a question of believing, James. It's how it is. You have to find a way to deal with it. It's not easy for me, either. Any of us.'

'What is it? A *curse*?'

'Maybe it's a blessing. I get to sing like Daisy.' Her smile was sad, sympathetic. 'We don't talk about this, James. All right? We just get on with our lives. You get used to it. I have to get ready, now.'

'But I used to be able to play fine. Now I can't even hold a tune outside of this stupid pub. How can I get used to it?'

'You had better. Our last trumpet player let it get to him. Wallowed in it. He's completely fucked up now.'

'I'm already fucked up!' He was shouting, pulling off his hat and twisting in his hands, as if it was the cause of his trouble. 'I'm stuck in this pub for how long? Forever?'

Sofia snorted, and turned to go. 'Just like the rest of us. Get over yourself, we're on in five minutes.'

James could not calm down. He went back into the bar, clutching his trumpet case and his crumpled trilby. He ordered a pint, but halfway through it he was seized with restlessness; it was intolerable to sit in the pub that was ruining his life.

Pushing the door open, he made it all the way to the door of his hostel. There was a lull in the pub noise behind him, and the opening phrase of 'Take the A Train' on the piano. He stood in the doorway, caught between feelings. The pub was hateful. It had drained his music away: either he was losing his mind, or the pub's past was consuming his future. Yet if he did not go in, he would lose his only chance to play music of any kind until the following weekend. Maybe forever, if they threw him out of the band for missing the gig.

James smoothed out the brim of his hat and walked back across the road to the Echo. A bewildered nymph stared down at him from the sign hanging above the door, paint peeling from the lettering of 'THE ECHO'.

As he stepped inside the pub, the band was already halfway through its first number. The singer fixed her large eyes on him through the crowd and beckoned him up to the stage. 'There you are! A big hand for our trumpet player, who's finally shown up. Come on, Jonny!'

Popping open the catches on his trumpet case, Jonny grinned, made his way through the applauding crowd, and took his place on stage beside Daisy Miller.

James had a flight home booked for noon on the day his visa expired. The night before, he packed his bag; he unpacked it again, and repacked it. As he set his phone's alarm, he noticed that the battery was getting low. He did not plug it in. Let it make the decision for him: if the battery lasted long enough to wake him in time, he would go. But though he could not sleep until the birds began their shrill chorus, he woke up at precisely the time his phone would have rung its alarm, had it not died. He lay immobile, opening his eyes every few minutes to see if the moment had passed.

He stayed all day in the hostel, his mind wearing itself out with the same set of thoughts on repeat. In the evening he sat in the little lounge with bowl of noodles in front of the TV. The news was full of a gathering mood of anger and frustration among the city's youth. Not far off, a couple of bus stops away in the adjacent borough, the police had opened fire on someone and killed him. Young men were out in the streets, smashing in windows and looting.

James paid little attention. The agitation in the streets seemed to reflect the rage building up in the pit of his own stomach, spreading out through his limbs. He had not left Rangewood and come halfway round the world just to get trapped again, this time with no chance to escape.

Images of the city's chaos succeeded each other on the TV screen: an overturned police car, young men swarming down a high street, a church blazing. From outside, there were sounds of breaking glass and shouting, and more distantly, police sirens, a plaintive edge to their undulation; the day was not going the police's way. Two German girls sitting opposite James on the sofa huddled closer together at the sound of the riot getting closer.

On an impulse, James stepped out of the hostel's front door and onto the street. There were people everywhere. The chemist shop had its window smashed, as did the beauty salon next to the Echo. A young man ran by with a strip of cloth pulled over his face like an old-fashioned bandit; he lobbed a brick through an upper window of the Echo. His eyes searched James' face for a second. 'What are you looking at?'

'Nothing,' said James, but the boy had already moved on, whooping and calling his friends to follow. James looked up at the window. The broken pane was a rupture in the pub's solidity, its timelessness.

Later, James would remember carrying out the idea before it had formed in his mind. He found himself wrapping his own scarf over his face, and walking in through the door of the service station, which was already half off its hinges.

There was no-one at the till, or anywhere in the shop. The fridge doors had been yanked open; cans of soft drink clattered around his feet as

James walked through the shop. He walked out again with a heavy can of petrol in either hand.

The bulk of the rioters had moved on up the street. But there was no sign of the police. James unstopped one of his petrol cans and threw it through the window of the pub. It rolled across the floor and stopped at the foot of the stage.

James hefted the other can and doused the Echo's door, its windowsills, its wall. When the can was almost empty, he smashed in the other window and tossed it across to join the other.

The smell of the petrol was strong in his nostrils. James took out his lighter; it took several flicks to get it started. He caught sight of a reflection in the window pane. It was Jonny's face he saw, distraught, shaking his head. Jonny's mouth opened in a silent plea.

There was something in that face, pale as the moon between its freckles, that gave James pause. Perhaps it was a warning, for James' sake as well as Jonny's own, not to destroy the one place James could still play music. The lighter grew hot between his fingers. In a moment it would burn his fingers, and he would drop it. The second decision he would have allowed to be made for him that day. With that thought, he snapped out of his confusion and pushed the flame onto the petrol-soaked window sill.

James backed into the road, watching the fire spread through the bar until it was visible in all the ground-floor windows. He felt the eyes of the other travellers watching him from the hostel windows. In between the sound of crackling flame and the pop of liquor bottles exploding from the heat, great gusts of melody burst out in waves of song and fountains of applause overlapping each other. Music, trapped for decades in the Echo's masonry, was foaming out and dissipating in the air.

The fire had spread to the upper windows. There, for a moment, Daisy Miller was visible, illuminated by the glow. She held up a hand in farewell, and he was not sure if it was with regret or relief that she was waving to him. Then flames engulfed the window and she was gone.

Be a Memory

Matthew Cai

Be a photogenic still
and not a refracted, dire-rapt memory.
Be unwavering and unravelled
for me in this kiss-like caressing, breathing:
a tangible moment
not to be questioned
until we're old and wise.

Let me absolve your murmuring dialogue
and other buildings of character or plot,
and for now replay a scene of us
loosely lying on the sun-dried grass
under the oak's speedy shadow.

Remain a stiff serving of wine
swigged heartily in any metropolitan bistro
and not a tongue-tied parley
with a nameless neighbour.
Study me with your brittle smile –
painted so delicately in this portrait,
and be those accompanied thousand words:
permanent and published.

Still Fishin' – Drew Rooke

In the Kingdom of Heaven

Tasneem Choudhury

Miras held his father's hand as they weaved their way through the crowd. The markets were always busy at this time of the day, even more so at this time of the year.

'*As-Salaam alaikum!*' *Peace be upon you!* Miras watched as his father embraced a tall man in the crowd.

'*Walaikum as-Salaam! Ramadan Mubarak!*' *And peace unto you! Happy Ramadan!* the man replied, 'Ah, and how are you Miras?'

Miras, embarrassed by the attention, hid behind his father who laughed off his shyness.

'Miras is just fine! He's just excited about Ramadan; he turned seven years old last month, this will be his first year fasting.'

'*Masha'Allah!*' *God has willed it!* praised the man, beaming as he tussled Miras' hair.

Miras and his father continued, having waved goodbye to his father's friend. The sun was directly above their heads at this time, but they were protected by the crisscrossing shade cloth draped over the roofs of the various stalls. The smell of mansaf wafted in from the food vendors and filled Miras's nostrils; he could almost taste the chewy cheesecloth yoghurt. Although, now that he would be fasting like his father, he would have to desensitise himself to the familiar fragrance. They had come to the market to stock up on food supplies for the week; Miras was looking forward to buying the dates in particular. He loved how such a little thing could carry in it so much sweetness.

As he and his father approached one of the date stalls, this one being owned by a friend of his father's, Miras noticed that their movement through the crowd was decreasing steadily. He peeked out from his father's shadow and spied the long lines of eager consumers which had formed at the stall. It was past midday, and the hordes had not relented; but it was to be expected. Usually, people do not move about so readily throughout the day; they fear to leave their homes unless it is necessary. In recent weeks, Miras had heard of the battles which had broken out nearby; he had heard the gunshots and the devastating sound of the falling shells. During Ramadan however, he noticed that people would seem happy; well, compared to how they seemed during the rest of the year. As they finally reached the stall, Miras' father exchanged pleasantries and a warm handshake with the vendor.

'Ah! What do you have for me Abbas?' Miras heard his father ask.

The man smiled.

'I have something special this time. Here!' exclaimed the man as he lifted the cover of a wicker basket filled to the brim with luscious dates. 'Fresh from Medina! Just got them three days ago. Here, try!'

Miras stood up on his toes, peeking over the counter, as his father grabbed two dates and handed one to him.

'What do you think Miras?' his father asked, still chewing.

Miras nodded excitedly with approval; the vendor laughed.

'Here Miras! I've got something for you,' the vendor exclaimed as he reached underneath the counter and pulled out a small, black toy gun, 'Ramadan Mubarak!'

Miras lit up at the sight of it; he didn't have too many toys, and neither did any of the other kids. The scarcity of it made it all the more valuable. Now he would not have to pretend that sticks were guns!

His father paid for a large bag of dates and shook hands with the vendor before the two set off again to navigate their way home.

The family lived in the Dheisheh Refugee Camp near Bethlehem along with fifteen thousand others. Miras had been born in the camp just like his father had been; it was all he knew. Even his grandfather was born there, but that was way back in 1948 when the camp was first established. The conditions in the camp were of course very poor; there were three under-resourced schools and five doctors to cater for everyone. However, things had improved. Miras remembered when they still lived in a large tent dwelling, and how the wind would sometimes burst through and knock things about. However after four long years, they had finally managed to build a proper house; it only had two small rooms which housed all six of them, but nevertheless, the solid walls were most welcome.

Miras's father kicked up sand as he walked. Miras watched as a light breeze came and ushered the sand away. His feet were tired; they had been at the market, walking and talking for over an hour. How he wished he could go and play soccer with Jamal and Wasim! He was too tired to walk, but not too tired to play.

The sun hit the roof of their house as it came into view; it was at the corner of the street, surrounded by narrow roads. In the distance, Miras could see the remains of what used to be the Ibdaa Cultural Centre. Miras liked the word *ibdaa*, it meant to create something out of nothing. His father had gone there when he was a child. He would tell of all the different games and activities which were available at the centre. However, that was long ago; the centre had been destroyed in a bombing raid more than two decades ago. At the time, his father told him the incident was labelled a 'mistake' by the occupying forces, but Miras wondered how you could *mistakenly* destroy a children's centre. On one of the crumbling walls of the building Miras's father had showed him a particular graffiti tag which ran across the remains of the wall. His father said it was written in English.

'Justice is what we need!'

Miras's father had told him that 'justice' was just another word for freedom. That made more sense to Miras.

As they entered the house, Miras saw his mother on the sofa, cradling his baby sister Bara in her arms. Bara, like him, like all of them, had been born in the Camp. She was still only eleven months old. Miras caught his mother's gaze as she smiled at him.

'Miras, you look tired! You should have a nap.'

'But I want to go and play with Jamal and Wasim!' pleaded Miras.

'But how will you be able to play if you don't have any energy? Go and rest first.' His mother answered sweetly.

She was right, thought Miras. For some reason, she was always right. He had heard it was because Heaven lay at a mother's feet; that mothers were blessed.

As Miras hauled himself onto the bed, he felt himself powerless as his eyes closed the doors to the world.

A loud crash permeated through the air; Miras was suddenly awake, and he was scared. He grabbed his toy gun which lay next to him to protect himself. He heard loud voices shouting; his father's was one of them.

'What is this? Why are you here?'

'Get down on the ground or else! There was a rocket fired from here; who was it?'

Miras crawled slowly up to the door and peeked around it, straining to get a better look. He saw three soldiers in the room and his father prostrate on the ground with his hands behind his head.

The soldier saw Miras, and the gun he was holding.

'The boy! Bring him along!' barked one soldier to the other.

'He's just a boy! Please, don't take him! He has done nothing! I swear it!' shrieked Miras's mother, grabbing the front of one of the soldier's jacket. The soldier recoiled and pushed her to the ground as she began to moan in pain; she could not bear the thought of Miras being taken away.

Miras began to move before he was quickly picked up and put upon the soldier's shoulder. The other two soldiers grabbed his father and dragged him out of the house. Miras, facing the house from the soldier's shoulder, could still see his mother through the entrance; she was still on the ground as Miras moved further and further away.

He was thrown into the back of the army vehicle; he cried out as he hit his head against its sides and slipped out of consciousness.

Miras awoke.

He felt two strong hands lift him up; he checked that the toy gun was still in his hand. It wasn't. He looked up; the sky was clear and the clouds were floating peacefully; the ear-splitting crackle of gunfire in the distance could not disturb him. He was put onto the ground; he could see his father, only metres away, lined up against a wall with other men. Miras brought himself up and looked at his father, tears flowing freely from his eyes. His father caught his gaze with his hands still behind his head; he smiled, hoping it would show above the expression of pain singed across his face and provide some comfort for Miras.

Miras saw his father smile; but there was no warmth in it, only fear. Then he watched as one of the soldiers pulled out a gun that resembled his own toy gun. The soldier calmly walked over to his father, and pointed the gun to his head.

Miras saw a flock of birds, doves perhaps, scatter as a loud BANG reverberated through the air.

Stranger

Martin Everett

There. Christ. Look what he's doing, he's so hyper, he never stops talking. The bloody phone is always at his ear.

What's going on?

Same time all this week. Okay, so I'm on the same train as well, bloody thousands of us are on the London underground this time in the morning. The same time as when the bomb went off. Jesus was it eight years ago already?

I have to get to know what's happening, there's something odd but I don't know what. I saw him on Monday in the same carriage as this, one back from the driver. I happened to get into it, I never plan which one to get in but he always gets into this one. He may have been coming on the train for weeks before I noticed, I can't remember when I have used this carriage before this week.

'Don't be Alarmed be Aware.' The posters are everywhere. I became aware of him on Monday but I don't know why.

I saw him on Tuesday edging through the crowd towards the far end of the platform. Phone held tight to his ear jabbering away but always looking around, not like he was looking for someone, but more like he was looking for someone looking for him. I got on behind him and watched as he carried on talking, I think he checked me out but I can't be certain.

Wednesday sealed it. Something is going on, the front carriage was totally full but he didn't come back along the platform to get into another one, he waited for the next train. I hung back and did the same. I don't think he noticed and I could not hear what he was saying as I did not want to get too close but he was even more animated than usual.

I got in the same carriage as him again today looking for something more definite in his behaviour to justify reporting him, the bombing anniversary is coming up perhaps there is a connection.

The train suddenly ground to a halt, and I panicked. The lights did not go out but they certainly dimmed. Did he have friends that had blown up other trains and is he going to blow this one? No; they would have coordinated the attack. He's still on the phone; strange he seems to be carrying on the conversation, I would have noticed if he had paused and surely he would have commented about the sudden stop no matter who he was talking to. Unless of course, whoever they are, is on the train as well. Well they're not in this carriage, no-one else is on the phone, maybe they're in a different one but then why not travel together if you're going to non-stop talk?

They must not want to be seen together for some reason. Was this the planning stage of something? Was our halt to do with it? Are they coming to arrest him?

The phone pressed into his ear he spoke into the mouthpiece, he had tried using bluetooth or plugging in earphones but for some reason he could make no sense of what he was hearing.

'I'm being watched, what shall I do? He thinks he's so smart but I saw him eyeing me on Monday, I don't want to be noticed. I thought I had the perfect cover, don't tell me it's blown already.'

'You're fine,' the voice replied. 'You're too clever to get caught.'

'Are you sure? He was in the same carriage as us on Tuesday, he kept glancing my way, and I was talking to you about what was the right thing to do. I didn't raise my voice, promise I didn't, so don't shout at me. Okay so I shouted a bit on Wednesday but can't you see the stress I was under? You told me I must use this carriage that's how I was sure he was on to me, the front carriage on first train was too full, I waited for the next and he did too.

Lately it's been great, no-one staring, I've been just a face in the crowd nothing to worry about. But here he is again. Now the train has stopped, has someone heard us? Are they after me?

'Calm down.'

'It's alright for you to say but it's me they'll get.'

'If they get you they'll get me too.'

We've been here for bloody twenty minutes he's still raving on. I wish I could ring the office but there's no coverage down here. Jesus! The meeting, I've got to ring the office, I forgot, I've been so tied up thinking about that guy I forgot to worry about the directors' meeting. If I don't contact them soon they are going to get really pissed. I'm struck by the thought no-one in the carriage had rung work with their excuse for lateness. Of course not you can't get through.

That's it! I know what's odd. He's the only one talking on the phone. It's strange but nothing to worry about, it's just he is always talking when no-one else can get coverage. I've got to find out who his provider is.

He's getting out of his seat and coming over what shall I do, it was working so well. The office doesn't know about my voices, you don't talk when I have to concentrate. I hated losing jobs when people saw me talking to thin air. Your idea to use a cell phone when I heard your voice was great, it made me look like all the other people talking to someone they can't see.

Even when we had a disagreement I could shout at you and no-one cared, I didn't get thrown out of pubs or even restaurants. I actually looked more important constantly being on the phone. Now we're blown. Does he work for the company? How did he find out? He is here. God he's agitated. No more like excited. What is he saying?

'Hey mate you've got to help me. No-one can get coverage down here. What network are you on? It must be fantastic.'

He's smiling, first time I've seen him really relaxed.

It's worked. It's worked! Even though I stood out he does not suspect I am talking to a voice that only I can hear.

But he's right in more ways than one.

'The network mate? It really is fantastic.'

To My Brothers

after John Keats

Erin Martine Sessions

My brothers retire to my balcony,
watch kookaburras rush from tree to tree,
remark upon the bamboo canopy,
and remember seventeen birthdays we
have shared in familiar company.
Ethan picks and plucks his ukulele.
Dad builds a barbeque. And what of me?
I recline and write this soliloquy:
This is your birthday Evan, and I pray
each one that follows will surpass the last
in the time we have with one another.
And as sunlight through our green ceiling fades,
foreshadowed are the birthdays yet to pass:
a lifetime of barbeques with my brothers.

The Pelican Wife
Thomas's Organ Morgans' Sunday Roost

Sarah Hilton

It was when the pelican wife said, 'But you've always been quite a little man, husband. That sort of thing has never suited you well. You know that as well as I do (o, quivering rabbit),' that he felt the knotted rope of anger snake, thickly, coilingly down his throat, and screw the bag of his stomach in a slow, rage-born tension.

The pelican wife sat across the low, claw-footed table, her great bill filled with a soup of malice. Really, what an ugly, noisy creature she is, he thought. He suddenly imagined, in that hushed twilight, the worn, old table's feet twitching, itching into life, catching her spindly ankle in its worn heeled boot, snatching her shrunken wrist, shaking her light frame until it fell with a flump onto the worn two-seater. Limp feather-down would spill from those dusty cushions and drift earthwards to shroud the furniture. The tall lamp would glow dully beneath its pleated shade.

'Husband! I'm speaking,' the pelican wife said. (O, nibbling minnow), he heard.

Her beringed fingers lay heavily in her hollow lap. *What if,* he thought in a fever, *what if those stacks of gold and navy sapphire were to animate, what if they were to drag one hand towards her monstrous bill, the other towards her sunken throat?* That cawing cadence would be forced back to a choked cry. And then he might rise, and take the tea tray to the kitchen. He might stand a moment by the sink, to inhale the silence and expel the sound of himself.

'... cardamom,' she was saying, 'and I want to bake it tonight. Husband, do listen. I tell you, don't I, tell you important things, but it's always something else with you, isn't it?'

He tugged an absent smile across his lips in agreement. Was it because of her black eyes, embedded in either side of her head, that her vision was fragmented, that shapes and colours gave meaning only in terms of the pelican herself? Safe flight, catch prey, safe flight.

'Well, be back before six, I want the ingredients together before dinner. I'll be upstairs, husband, and goodness do I have a headache. I know I didn't have it before afternoon tea, either, and I've told you countless times to watch the pot, haven't I: two and a half minutes for black, four minutes for chamomile. Oh,' and she raised two mottled talons to her temple, 'my head'. Nobly weak, momentarily, like the veteran stage actress with the crowd encased under the clean white feathers of her wing. 'I'm going to take a little nap, husband. Make sure you wake me as soon as you get back, and remember about the black tea, I tell you important things and you're just – '

(O, flailing salmon husband), he heard in the sigh of the sofa as she rose. He waited. After a moment, even creaks, like whistling breaths, reverberated through the plaster as her strong flat feet ascended the stairs. As the pelican wife's footsteps rose to pace the ceiling above his head, he felt the coil of anger loosen to sit, slackly, in his abdomen, but still he imagined the room. He saw the four posts of the bed folding in at once, like an octopus, a stiff, lumbering quadruped of his own creation, smothering her with laundered bed sheet and embroidered quilt, the wooden posts as a trap of crossbones from which the struggling, monstrous beak protruded comically. He could discern the distant rustling and creaking as she made her nest comfortable.

Cardamom, cardamom. For the Sunday cake, of course, the Sunday cake. He felt like a child feigning a sophisticated palate when he ate her cardamom cake, warm and unchallenging in look and texture, a foreign land when he took a clumsy mouthful. The spice filled his senses with bittersweet perfume, until he couldn't detect whether he was engaged by taste or smell. Did the parts make the whole? Was the whole only a plan of her invention? Perhaps he wouldn't eat it this time, anyway, he thought. He only chewed to dam with rolling logs the singing brook of her chatter, to net the silvery fish.

Down the narrow hallway, then, like a familiar dream. Bulbs dimming, must take them down, buy more. Battered reed organ clung to the wall, lid a cluttered herd of photographs. He paused absently to dust the frame that enclosed their daughter as a child, and to cast a knotted hand over the sleeping keys. Soft tread on the imitation Persian runner, quiet jingle of key from the coat hook.

The door stuck in the summer humidity, as always. He performed the code-like ritual: a handle-turn, a lift up and to the right. A tap with a leather-bound toe. A gritted-teeth push with the heel of his other hand until it gave way. His breath came fast (as it did at strange times, nowadays; whether it was from bearing the words of the pelican wife or struggling with the door, or the effort of swapping his slippers for shoes, he would never know). He felt himself quite exhausted by the time he emerged on the other side of the mottled garden gate. The wrought iron screamed through the silent summer evening as he slowly bent over and latched it shut. He could already hear the pelican wife's surge of streaming cries if next door's terrier were found among her azaleas.

The Chinese man at the grocery shop grinned at his request. His spotted olive hands swiftly slung the dried pods into a plastic bag. 'Cardamom again! Your wife, always making cardamom! Too much! Too much cardamom!' The man accepted the small note – no change, of course, cultivation of cardamom is labour-intensive and very expensive, but worth it to some. 'You got to stop her one day, you know!'

His throat was closed with disuse. He coughed quietly (the only way he knew how). 'I will, one day.'

Now the hushed twilight had been swallowed by silent dark, but he wasn't in fear of a scolding. The iron gate moaned in beautiful resonance as he pushed it open. The door again in reverse, now: key slid in, up, to the left, tap with the foot, hammer with the right hand. The familiar dream of the hallway unchanged in twenty years, the imitation Persian runner which ribboned up the stairs, up, up the stairs with quiet step, rustling plastic bag, to the door of her bedroom.

The bedposts stood solid, the quilts a disturbed pool. Her face was still. Her wide brown hands were spread unnaturally, one lying at her chest and one grasping a handful of bed sheet. He studied the parted wings of her dull white hair. Not dead – no, no! this isn't that sort of story – but adrift in the sleep of the green dreamed sea deeps.

He softly, softly set down the bag, and sank his old frame into the sheets beside hers. He clasped her limp arm in his warm hand. He was, after all, a man who had always loved his wife. (O, strong sailing pelican mine), he said.

Creatures of the Vineyard

Elisabeth Murray

Yes, it shames us to think we didn't pay Mrs Pope any mind. She was a bow-legged creature smelling of old milk and when she took to screeching at the town meetings about her beans disappearing we listened as we would to Mr Mather, we are always polite, and then got on with the agenda. Poor Mrs Pope. Someone the other evening made a motion to get up a statue of her on the main street. Engraved with something like: 'listen to your old people'. Sometimes the voice of the Lord comes through the lips we least expect. We should have had sentries over her garden, armed. As it was she took to sitting on her veranda after dark and her eyes being what they were she caught young Newt Cheever with a bullet from her husband's hunting rifle.

Newt pulled up fine, just a piece out of his shoulder. His mother resented more that he'd been late for dinner and had the hide to cut through Mrs Pope's yard. We made a joke of it and the beans that started the fuss had no part in the remembering. It was only in time to come that we speculated that Mrs Pope must have dropped off over her sherry while the beans vanished, that it was far more insidious than anything young Newt could occasion. There are kinds of depravity you cannot measure by your own code. There are things that must be done that a town like ours can hardly find heart to do.

Abe Lawson was the first to see them. He was working late in the vineyards and there they were sitting in one of the rows. He said he could have picked them up and snapped off their limbs as you would a bad part of a vine and if only he had. When he told us they had a greenish tinge to their skin like the sea from far off we laughed and went back to our yarns and our tipples but Abe's eyes bulged like planets and he spoke as if his voice was being chased out of him. We thought *not another one for the asylum, not Abe.*

He took Officer Braybrook and Cannonball Putnam, for the guns, but there were no shots. Whether it was the lure of the hideous or just plain pity is difficult to tell. It's in that first instant that we leave ourselves wide open. You can't blame Officer Braybrook and Cannonball. The Devil catches us unawares and weren't we all stripped of our reason in the days that followed? Every soul in town trooped in to clap eyes on them.

That night we gathered in the courthouse square. Mr Mather was away at his summer house so we took our courage from the lamplight that was like the gaze of our forefathers. Free as our kindness was that night none of us was foolish enough to offer our own roof. Jed Abbey had some room at his inn but his wife had just scrubbed it spotless. Besides, Jed was one of the most flustered, he stood shaking and pale under the lamp.

Finally the barracks on Terminer Street were suggested. Yes, they are the pride of the town but courtesy is our deepest urge for better or worse. Every passer-through is hailed and clapped on the back and taken in for sandwiches and tea. It goes to show the vileness of the creatures that we didn't meet them like that, but if you know how we cherish our barracks you'll know our core is goodwill.

The creatures sat against the wall of the quarters in their cocoon-coloured material as though they could not discern such marks of civilisation as beds. The place had a strange smell as if a rat had crawled into a gap and died. Something about the way they sat close together made someone remark that they might be children. Someone suggested one of us ought to stay with them but somehow that didn't eventuate.

We stood before the building: long, flat, the colour of larvae but for the gunpowder-dark windows. There was no sign of anything untoward. But little else than goodbye was said as we reached our houses in turn and we knew it would be a sleepless night for all of us.

All was quiet next morning. Any shops that were open were presided over by a red-eyed soul drinking cup after cup of coffee. Any stranger who chanced to arrive that day would think we had been cursed.

We watched Abe bring the creatures bread, apples, stew – perfectly decent, mind you, Virgie Lawson is no layabout – and we watched them turn to the wall and whimper like dogs. Newt piped up that we ought to try beans. Officer Braybrook, about to cuff the boy around the head, had to turn the blow to his own. It so happened they swallowed them down like the bread of life. Some wiseacre chipped in later, after everything, that obviously beans were the food of the dead. We were all struck dumb, but why should we have thought of that? The Devil does most of his work on unsuspecting folk. It is easy to cast aspersions once destiny is told.

When the beans were finished one of them snatched up the plastic and tore out a piece like an animal too savage to isolate the good meat. It spat it out with a whine and saliva swung off its face. Officer Braybrook began to sidle towards them. We held our breath. The one with the saliva put its arms around the other.

'Too dumb to move,' said Newt and Cannonball Putnam seized his head under his arm so Newt gazed out like an owl.

The officer took another step and said, 'Where are you from?' His voice was vast in the cold room. The creatures did nothing but huddle there mewing.

'Come on, where are you things from?' He raised his voice as though perhaps the only trouble was that they could not hear him. 'We've put a roof over your heads, we've fed you, we've been very lenient. Least you can do is thank us.'

They were looking up by the time he finished but gave no sign they would answer. Officer Braybrook is a fine man, but one trait that does not belong to him is patience. He strode out of the building with his fists gritted and his face black. People pushed to the front. In those first days anyone would have thought a freak show had come to town and was being exhibited in our barracks.

It was little Dolly Phips who got them to speak. That is not the word, but the Lord has given us this dictionary and it was not prepared for such vagaries. Such hoarse, wet noises as if the creatures themselves were ashamed of their tongues. Dolly knelt down before them, poor simple child. They must have seen how simple. She was as blonde as a buttercup. Though they spoke only once and Addie Toothaker had the sense to pull her back the gobbledegook put shivers down our spines. Dolly's mother almost broke when she heard what happened and forbade her to go within a mile of the place. But an unholy prayer is like a match dropped in a vineyard.

They spoke to nobody else, only sat there as though they'd come to the coldest place on Earth. We thought *none of us bullied you into coming.*

They became like an indecent fresco we didn't know how to get rid of. If only Abe or Officer Braybrook or Cannonball had shot them at the outset. It is harder to shoot a thing at close range, no matter how inhuman.

The Devil waits for such a hush. We were guards who had drifted into sleep, not seeing menace in shadows at the crust of our territory. One evening there was a downpour that sounded like an army coming in from the hills. We stood on our porches looking through a curtain the colour of aluminium. Cannonball on his way back from Abbey Inn drove into the Lawsons' mailbox. Dolly Phips ran in from her backyard and her hair was plastered to her face and her dress to her legs. The worst of it was that it was as cold as death. Venture to poke your finger out the window and you would be sucking it warm half the night. Poor Dolly was living – almost dying – proof of that. A second in that deluge and she was in bed a week. Lucky it wasn't from there straight to the coffin, Doctor said. The downpour lasted not a night but when a town, as close-knit a town as we were then, is cooped up separate with such a terrible spectacle going on it is as good as being shut in a cell. Even sitting by our husband or wife or grandchildren the water was so that we had to shout to be heard. In as gentle a town as ours!

Next day we woke to a glare like spring at our curtains but tore them back to find a tableau of snow. It was no picture book eiderdown. At the side of the road it was like oatmeal left too long. It dripped from the roofs. It was summer and that day we looked like tourists, our winter clothes still creased, unsuited to a snowscape. Even old Mr Cory stood at his door shaking his head and he has seen all manner of things happen twice over in this town.

We are not a suspicious people. But would you turn a blind eye if practically the next day it was so humid you thought you'd been transported to a savage rainforest? How was it the sky hadn't unburdened itself the night of the deluge? We were drenched and speechless, like fish.

So it was plain: these were no maladjusted children. No offensive fresco. The barracks looked like an ancient ruin after such extremes. The sandstone was dark, somehow expanded, as though it had ingested the rain and frost and now the humidity was a seal. The cross stood like a neon stick in the sun. And though we stood well back there was a smell of mildew, acridly sweet, like a pear forgotten in a bag. In our three days of hardship the creatures became true monsters. Green as mould, demon-ugly, with a ravenous bigotry and the power to do something about it.

Then a different kind of demon came. A distraction dangled by the Devil, in a car the colour of washing powder and a suit that matched. He was fat and sweated. He had heard of our little difficulty and his men were doing all they could. We said, 'What do you plan to do with them, *sir*?' And he said, 'Well of course they will be kept for a time in your barracks as you call them, which we will make liveable, and once they have proved harmless, once they have learned enough of how we do things, they will be set loose.' He took half an hour to say it, but that was the gist.

We demanded he face us at a town meeting and he looked at us crowded there fit to be tied, went back to his car and talked on a phone and came back and said, 'I suppose that would be possible.' And sweated.

The evening was the colour of ash and as hot. Everyone looked as though they had stepped out of a creek. The hall had never been so full. Children were awake on Coca-Cola, swinging their legs and fidgeting. We watched the platform with eyes that appeared inhuman, unsoftened by sleep.

He lifted himself out of his chair and hauled up to the lectern. He sweated and talked like a bad salesman. He was right to be afraid.

'When did this become a dictatorship? When?'

'Sir, if you will listen to my argument –'

'These are aliens!' called Gerty Porter who teaches our youngsters.

The fat man said, 'I wouldn't call them that –'

'Living right next door to people who are decent, who've done nothing to deserve this! Oh, our poor children.'

'It seems to me you are describing some form of mythical creature –'

'Have you bothered to take a look at them before you started with your bleeding heart meddling?'

'Of course sir, and they –'

'Mister, what about us?' Abigail Fisk stood with her back rigid, chin raised. She always wins the prizes at the high school. 'You're making sure these aliens are safe, what about *us*?'

There was applause and shouts of, 'yeah, what about us?' The fat man stood blinking sweat out of his eyes.

'I assure you, you will be compensated. You may even find that you are better off as these immigrants enter your community.'

'Over our dead bodies,' yelled Cannonball and many echoed, 'Yeah! Our dead bodies!'

'We've worked our guts out for our houses, and you're telling us these aliens get one free of charge?'

'It is not a house –'

'I notice you haven't brought any razor wire with you.'

'No, that's slightly old-fashioned –'

'Why not put up a picket fence while you're at it?'

'Sir, it is only a form of shelter –'

'What the hell are we going to tell our children when they can't go out and play in the street?'

Many were in tears now and all the fat man could say was, 'Now, I don't think that's quite true.' Gerty Porter kept sobbing, 'Think of our poor children.' He said it was getting late but he would take our concerns to his men and as he went out to his car Cannonball told him he could take *this* to his men and tried to crack him over the head with a placard but someone caught him and patted his arm and said there were better ways to fight.

We went home in the hot black night that reeked of the Devil. A few of our men stayed late at Abbey's Inn and then got their guns and staggered into the night sweating with whisky but the fat man had stolen out of town. One of them shot into the air and it rang like a plea.

The smaller monster grew uglier. Its face seemed greener. It spluttered up patches of some dark substance. We wondered, might there burst even from these creatures something like blood? We were thrown into panic that this was another phase of their malediction. With relief we understood. Its chest was like a birdcage under the material. It lay on its back, even in illness unable to see the function of a bed. When it died the other one howled but it faced the point of the gun and the blast that stilled it was not only sound but matter, a spray of blood on the wall like an unspeakable stain on a fresco.

That night it seemed to cool and we slept sounder. We know we did wrong in that. If there is blame for us anywhere it is in our sleep. Keep one eye open always and a hand on the weapon.

Towards noon when the heat had revived Abe came flying down the road. There were more this time and they seemed larger, more hideous, the way a bearded lady is a novelty until she cracks and takes up an axe through the town. Then you wouldn't invite any wench with whiskers into your home no matter how unlike, would you? This time we didn't hesitate. Half-eaten chickens, half-drunk wine left to warm. Letty Danforth left her hairdressers' wide open and one of the hairdryers set fire to the place. She swears she turned it off. Couldn't we have one moment of respite?

They were thrown into the barracks and nobody was rushing for a glimpse. By now it was plain these monsters, aliens, agents of the Devil, whatever they were, could not have been getting in without aid. A City of God is impregnable unless weakened from the inside. Suddenly our home was disfigured by shadows. Where the porches had looked golden now if there was someone rocking and sipping there you had an instinct to avoid their gaze.

We had thought the downpour, snow, and swelter was curse enough. We'd thought we were whittled down to our spines by sleeplessness. Then there came a blow straight to our essence: fungus on the grapevines. Powdery mildew or oidium it was, and it strangled like hatred. It had the look of the stuff on a newborn, but it was the down of death. When Mr Mather returned from his summer home he strode to his most beloved slope and took a solitary grape between his thumb and forefinger without breaking it from the vine. Then he sank to his knees. In his cashmere suit. When he stood he was composed, the fury buried in his face. He gave his orders then.

The town hall was reborn to us that evening. No prying fat men. This was ours, we knew what was needed. Jed said he'd just like to know how Abe had come across the creatures, he wasn't saying there was anything peculiar about Abe being the only soul up there that night, he'd just like to know. Letty said she'd read enough crime stories and wasn't it always the way, the guilty one was the first to proclaim the crime?

Abe wasn't at the meeting but by eight o'clock there wasn't a person didn't believe he'd smuggled in the Devil's servants.

Judge Hathorne's sentence was like a stage light in the courthouse, shining the narrow path to remedy. We were a congregation of sore eyes, swimming heads, lifeless bearing – and then it was revealed.

We gathered on the Common. It was blazing green that day, pretty as needlepoint. The lake was blue as a little girl's eye. The swans clustered at the bank under the willows.

The stones came slow and then swift. We went home with our skin stinging pink and it was still so hot we ate sandwiches and Coca-Cola inside with the doors shut and the curtains drawn.

The spell of relief was false as a treacherous neighbour. More of the demons and it was clear Abe hadn't been the only one colluding with the Devil. You have never seen a place where terror and sorrow were twisted in such a grisly braid. Snarled, blood-hardened. There was no wine to dull it. We were like another species ourselves, blurred by sleeplessness. For all we knew our neighbour or aunt or baker was one of those who'd invited the Devil in.

It is difficult to say who first accused who. So many agreed in a flash. They had always thought, now that it was mentioned, they had witnessed something not quite right. Poor Jed Abbey, poor Mr Cory, poor Letty Danforth, poor Mrs Pope. Poor us, who saw our town torn asunder and spared no effort to mend it.

We had lost our lifeblood, the vineyards and our intimacy. Our town may as well have been a metropolis for the cold between us. And the monsters that had brought this were cooked for by a troupe of city folk who had seen a thousand freaks and wouldn't know a servant of the Devil if they pushed sponge cake into its mouth.

We talked of leaving. But when we saw Mr Mather standing on the slopes like a holy vision we knew we could not betray him. It wasn't enough to band together. The Devil had laid his seed. For all we knew the neighbour with whom we plotted had signed her name in the Devil's book. By that time there was no helping the hardest blow. Perhaps we needed razor wire to keep our own out, not to keep the aliens in.

The children found their way inside. The Lord knows what happened to them in there. Little Dolly came running down the main street where the shutters were being lowered and the smells of cooking were spreading. The poor child hadn't been right since her spell in the downpour. The look was in her. Some of us fell to our knees before she spoke. She was saying, 'They were crying, mama, I saw them cry!'

The poor child. The Common dimmed at sunset like a slowly closing eye, anticipating peace. There was righteousness in our palms, smooth blocks of it. We felt the retreat of the Devil in the very arc of our arms, the way the reality of the world retires as you drift into sleep.

The Still Cricket

Daniel Zwi

There's a cricket sitting on a picture frame above my toilet. It's been there since the day before yesterday. It looks steadfastly down at me as I piss and I worry that it's preparing to jump at me, and if it did jump then I'd flinch mid-flow and spray urine all over the bathroom, including that disgusting area behind the toilet bowl which never gets cleaned; that neglected area where detached pubic hairs gather and middle-of-the-night misdirected urine congeals; except that this time I'd have to clean it up because it wouldn't just be a few wayward drops but a veritable lake. Imagine if the cricket landed on my cock, it doesn't bear thinking about. So I rush in and rush out, force the urine out my bladder like a juice presser squeezing oranges. I feel my abdominals tense and my sphincter tighten and my stream hits the far wall of the toilet bowl and ricochets upwards onto the seat, but at least I leave the bathroom unharmed.

Admittedly, there is another reason why I don't like the cricket. I can't shake the feeling – and I know it's irrational – that it's looking down at me and judging. Like when you're in a public toilet and the person next to you takes a sneaky glance at your cock (I don't want to get holier than thou about it because I've been known to do it too; that involuntary glimpse as you do your fly up and step backwards – the id rearing its ugly head in some Darwinian need to take stock of male competition, or otherwise in some suppressed homoerotic urge – it's probably both). Anyway, I feel that same self-consciousness in front of the cricket. It's not specifically about size. I'm not worried that the cricket thinks I'm small. On the contrary, it probably thinks that I'm phenomenally well-endowed, seeing as the length of my penis is two or three times its body size, even flaccid. No, it's more the general feeling of being watched that puts me off; the unpleasantness of knowing that you're being appraised as you let nature take its course. Pissing's become a gauntlet.

I remember playing aeroplanes with my father when I was younger. Before getting into the bath in the evenings, us both standing over the toilet; him pissing, me peeing (children don't piss), our jets crossing paths on their way to the bowl, sometimes an X-shape and sometimes a plus sign depending on how far apart we were standing. His was yellow and wide (the stream, I mean), losing its tension towards the toilet bowl and spreading out like shotgun fire. Mine was thin, clear and taut, like a laser beam. His the body of the aeroplane, mine the wings. His usually lasting much longer: I remember being amazed by the sheer volume of liquid being expelled from his body at one time. Mine ended abruptly, without drips, whereas his would always conclude with insipid secondary spurts after the main stream finished, like earthquake aftershocks. 'One day, you'll have to do this too', he'd said to me once, giving it a shake.

It could be my imagination but the cricket seems to be changing colour. It's going from green to dirty brown, a little browner each time I see it. The day before yesterday it looked healthy, its exoskeleton avocado-flesh green. I'd go as far as to say that it looked virile; an alpha male cricket lazily surveying its bathroom kingdom from atop the picture frame, its Pride Rock. But by yesterday it had lost some of its lustre. It kept more still, its body slightly darker. And today it's an earthy green colour, the colour of eucalyptus leaves. It has a waxen quality. When I got out of bed this morning and stood at the toilet, I wasn't scared of the cricket jumping at me so much as it falling on me, so insipid did it appear. Its only movement was the slow swaying of its two long antennae every few seconds.

It was during my last trip to the toilet, about half an hour ago, that it occurred to me that the cricket might be slowly starving to death. The bathroom has no bugs or plants in it and no window; God knows how it found its way in there in the first place. The walls are white and sterile; there's scarcely a cobweb. There's nothing for it to eat, this cricket, now that I think about it, and suddenly its mien is shifting from one of menace to one of vulnerability. Maybe I'm watching it die – that's why it's changing colour. Its stillness isn't as insidious anymore.

But if I'm right about it starving to death, I wonder why the cricket didn't leave the picture frame earlier in search of food or water, instead of waiting around in the bathroom until it was too weak to move elsewhere. Why didn't it venture down the drain or drink the toilet water, or fly (do crickets fly?) out of the bathroom and into our living room, with its dark corners and windows, where catching an insect or escaping into the great outdoors would have been a matter of course? Maybe it had been looking for food in the days before I saw it, had inadvertently wandered further and further away from where insects were likely to be, and, too exhausted to continue, decided on that spot above the toilet as its final resting place. Maybe by the time I saw it it had already given up hope.

Or perhaps it's been sitting there because it laid eggs nearby and needs to keep them warm and guard them. Its offspring may even need the body of the cricket to feed on once they hatch – maybe it's their only source of food. I saw a David Attenborough documentary recently where an octopus starved to death in this rocky crevice under a coral reef, protecting its eggs from intruders and providing meat for the hungry hatchlings. They used a time lapse camera over the course of a month, and the octopus, which started off bone-white with bright red streaks, grew greyer, more transparent, brittle, and thinner, thinner, thinner, until it died. It starved to death with monk-like acceptance; it didn't complain at all. There were all these scales, or skin cells, clouding the water around the octopus by the end of the time lapse; I guess it had started to disintegrate.

Watching that octopus dying, I remember being struck by the beauty of its uncompromising devotion to its offspring, but also slightly sobered by the realisation that a mother's love for their child is fundamentally instinctual, biologically mandated, mechanical. I remember worrying that its very inevitability cheapens that maternal dedication, like when you're a kid and your friend hurts you, and their mother says, 'Say sorry to Dan', and they say 'Sorry Dan', and you're grateful for your friend's apology but all the same, they didn't have a choice in the matter.

There was a time – and I stopped thinking this long before I saw the octopus documentary – when I thought that unbounded maternal love was a Jewish thing. It's embarrassing to admit that now, but at the time all I had to go by was my own mother's demonstrative love for me, and my (almost uniformly Jewish) friends' mothers' similarly demonstrative love of them – which, combined with the stereotype of the doting, overbearing Jewish mother (we complained about being stifled but secretly loved the attention) led me to believe that the strongest, gooiest form of maternal love was exclusive to the Jews. Of course, now I know it's not a Jewish thing. It's not a middle-class thing, it's not a white thing, it's not even a human thing. In a sense, it's not an animal thing. Any living organism has as its highest priority the survival of its offspring. So when I think back to my mum cleaning my mattress after I'd wet the bed at six or seven years old, or wiping the bathroom floor after I'd missed the toilet on school mornings, it's not that I don't appreciate it, or feel that she did it begrudgingly, or doubt the sincerity of her devotion – it's all genuine. I just think that she couldn't help being like that, any more than I can help finding beautiful women attractive or pain unpleasant. Maybe the cricket's like my mum, deferring to its maternal instinct by slowly rusting above the toilet in my bathroom. I'm going to check for its eggs next time I go in. The last thing I need is a swarm of crickets emerging from behind the picture frame while I'm trying to take a shit.

Millions

Neil Varcoe

This is silent country. The earth is burned red by the fierce sun. Dust rises up in clouds around his wheels as Jack's sulky HQ argues through the gears on the lonely stretch of highway between the city and the bush. It's no-man's-land, this place, nothingness, the never-never, a repeating landscape pocked by the occasional landmark, a burned-out car perhaps, the road littered by the pancaked remains of animals more suited to his country than him, that didn't make it. The road ahead was unclear, heat rose in waves, but Jack had driven it a thousand times and was on autopilot. This time of the year is usually filled with excitement, coming home to see the old man, jumping on bikes to round up cattle, marking them with the McMullen brand and herding them into trucks for sale. But Jack had a queasy feeling about this year's fortunes, perhaps due to his father's distance on the phone earlier that week. He had a feeling in his bones that this year was going to be different.

Their lot was in wild country. The sun was hot as hell and blowflies the size of footballs tried relentlessly to escape it, settling on your shadow, banging against your eyes, ears, climbing inside your mouth. A serpentine river worked its way through their property, sometimes like an arriving saviour in the wet and other times, a constant reminder of how little time they had for it to fill up with water so they could feed the thousands of cattle that stood on spindly legs, with barely the energy to move. Jack knew by regular checks of their stock numbers on his iPad that there had not been a new steer in twelve months, maybe more. Technology was one thing he had brought to the farm, but maybe these so-called game changers are not enough to beat this country. Perhaps his new way of thinking, 'Farming 2.0' as his father put it, was not enough to win the battle of taming the land, a war waged evermore bitter since before Eve bit the apple.

Jack cut a hard right into the family stake and his body shook like death as he crossed the cattle grate. He urged the ute onwards, gently, as he started the ten-minute drive along a straight dirt road to the homestead, the trusty old yellow trailer bouncing around behind him like an excited dog moments from home.

Jack had little idea what awaited him.

'Why not do up one of the old cars in the shed?' Jack said to his old man, his rake-thin arms on his hips, the two men looking like versions of the same man, one young, the other, 'mature'.

'What's wrong with fixing up an old box trailer, Millions?' he replied, 'The city's turned you into a poof.'

The kids at Jack's boarding school in the heart of the city used to call him Millions due to a terrible mistake he had made on the very first day of year seven. He was young and dumb and out to impress. A couple of the *real* country lads from large properties in remote areas, who had town cars and a city wardrobe and milk frozen in blocks in large industrial freezers because it was too far to town to grab a litre on a whim, were standing around talking about home and how big their lot was.

Jack busted into the group keen to make his mark, the hero of his imaginings made real.

'That's nothing,' he said, after one grain-fed boy told them his parents had a thousand acres.

Jack's face set into corrugations, which meant he was serious.

'That's nothing,' he repeated, this time with an air of the showman about him.

'My dad has *millions* of acres and so many cattle all you can see is horns, as far as the eye can see!'

The group fell silent and looked at each other, bewildered. They spewed laughter and burst out on their own to tell everyone in the schoolyard about their new mate, Millions McMullen.

Jack cast a wicked eye back at his old man and knew he was beat. He would never live that one down and nor should he, thought Jack.

'Beer?' his father said.

'I'm not here for a haircut,' Jack shoots back.

'Shame. You could do with one.'

The box trailer is a mute yellow like sunlight through dirty glass, its paint flaking like a drover's nose. The wheels are flat and cracked from the pressure put on them by staying in the same spot too long and the bolts, which are coupled with an assortment of nuts of all shapes and sizes, are rusted on like barnacles on the hull of a sunken ship. The sides are higher than they should be, thick wire welded to the original structure. It was altered to carry his father's things to university in the seventies, and back to the farm after he dropped out to run it just a few months later. Jack's father and his grandfather worked on the trailer as a project, welding their own bond through its construction, and painting over cracks caused by years of neglect. Now Jack was home from university to help out after the worst drought in forty years had dried up their funds, forcing his father to bump the ten remaining workers on their remote cattle farm, just in time for the annual roundup, the family's cash cow.

Jack knew that he would not be able to return to his studies if they did not find a way to make some money and fast, but this was the last thing his dad wanted to talk about.

'Remember that huge salty that used to stalk up and down the river over there, pinching full grown beasts from the banks like they were calves?' He said from his chair on the verandah, pointing across the front yard to the dusty arteries of old rivers that lay beyond the fence line, an ever-present reminder of the hell that they were in.

Jack follows the line of his fingers with his eyes and nods solemnly.

'That croc was the inspiration for the monster in that horror movie set up here about that American writer who came to capture that wild unpredictability, that rawness that they love so much about us. *Well, he got it alright!* I think the poor bastard lost an arm! That *raw* enough for him, ya reckon?'

'That was just a movie, Dad.'

His father pauses, tilts his head to the side and scrutinises the air as though someone wrote the answer on it. *Nope.* He powers on.

'Anyway, that big handbag was based on Old Salty. But when they took the bugger to the studio – in script form mind you, he doesn't have the patience or the inclination for travel – they baulked at the idea! He can't be that big! No-one is going to believe a croc *that* size lives in the Australian outback and goes about eating people! Well he does! Well, he lives here at least, or used to. There are not many people around here anymore for him to feast on, even the black fellas have moved into town.'

His dad stops and peers into his can of Fourex, surprised to see it has been drained. He punches his hand into the biting cold of the icebox and starts on another. He avoids Jack's eyes and looks out over the yard, which he has kept green with the last of the bore water. The vanity. He thinks to himself, *I will leave here, too, sooner, rather than later. One thing I won't do is string this noose around Jack's neck. I won't burden him under this yoke.*

'You got a missus, yet?' Jack's father said, disappearing into his tinnie, a smile on his lips like he had just baited a trap and was waiting for the bastard animal to finally trip up.

'Have you?' Jack said.

'Why would I need one of them, when I've got you to nag me and brush my hair when I'm sad and tell me everything is alright?'

'Very PC, Dad.'

'You on about those computers again, you're like a bloody broken record.'

Jack looked at him unsure whether he was making a joke. He thought it was best to say nothing than risk walking into another ambush.

'Okay, next topic,' his dad said, rolling below the old trailer to check the underbelly. The bottom of it looked like it should be the top, all thick steel and armour and ugly enough to ward off any predator.

'Playing footy?'

'Socially for a local side and college. We're horrible.'

'Good to hear some things never change.'

The two men did little talking for the next few hours, circling around the rusty old trailer, pointing at things, kicking and poking things, skinning their knuckles, the blood mingling with oil on the red earth as another tool went flying into the transport shed, blamed for whatever mistake the hand had made.

The sun burned red in the sky like a tired eye and the men decided it was time to quit for the day.

They cleaned and collected their tools, including the pile against the shed.

Jack's dad offered to put them away, while Jack started on dinner. It was very unlike him to do that.

His father hunted through the channels on the old His Master's Voice television as though he was actually looking for something.

He stopped on the ABC News.

The screen showed a mob of angry protesters marching on a city street angry at, well, just about everything gauging by the disparate slogans on their scrawly placards.

'The great unwashed,' his dad said. 'Bet they're all gays and vegetarians,' he continued, before stuffing half a rissole in his mouth.

'Very PC Dad.'

One protester, who unfortunately seemed to fit his father's description, burst into view, taking up the entire frame with a sign that read, 'SAY NO! TO GENETICALLY-MODIFIED FOOD! SAY NO! TO MUTANTS!'

His father almost choked on his food in a bid to give flight to his rebuff.

'You know what pisses me off?'

'I'm sure you're going to tell me.'

'These bloody hen-pecked libertines, who were obviously breastfeed until they were twelve, complain about wealth inequality, gay marriage, high taxes, whaling, land rights, land rights for gay whales, the list goes on!'

He throws his head back repeatedly in quick succession to move the food down into his gullet like a kookaburra swallowing a snake.

'But when it comes to looking after our own, they go missing.'

'How so?' Jack said, indulging the old man.

'This GM business, the push for so-called ethical farming and organic produce is making us all go bust.' He slammed down his fork.

'The earth is bone-dry and with the cost of upgrading our practices every five minutes, no wonder all the cockies are topping themselves.'

'Dad! Where did you learn the word "libertine?"'

His father shoots him a sideways glance, a kind of tap to the chin, more warning than knockout blow.

'Most of the people live in cities now, yet every time we seek to define ourselves internationally at some such thing, we roll out the kangaroos, Akubras and "G'day mates!"'

Jack stares straight ahead.

'We are a country who romanticises life on the land and bemoans farmers when they ask for help in hard times. You wonder where they think their food comes from?'

'Coles,' Jack answers.

His father looks over, provoked, and notices his son is not joking.

'Guess you are right. Maybe we should install a webcam so they can see where their "hundred percent Australian beef" comes from?'

'You're not as thick as you would have us believe, old fella,' Jack said, snatching the remote.

'Let's watch something without homosexuals or herbivores. We don't want you having a heart attack.'

Jack switches over to a soapie about a shiny group of twenty-somethings, who play school-aged girls and boys, set on the beach.

'Ah,' his father said, 'the other great Australian myth.'

Jack rises well before dawn and heads to the kitchen for a quick cup of tea before heading out. He rinses a dirty camping mug piled on top of a stinking pile of cups, plates and whatever else.

Something's gotta give, he thought.

He pushes the four-wheeler around to the front from the backyard via a small side gate and walks it about five hundred metres down the road before kicking it over, careful not to wake his father. He crawls along the fence line until he reaches a large gate. Jack unhitches the chain and wreathes it open – tall tufts of grass have grown around its feet. Now out of earshot, he guns the farm bike and follows the dried creek bed out into the heart of the property.

Where are all the animals?

He pulls the bike up at one of the old dams and dismounts. He wanders up to the edge and stares into the barren hole, the face of it cracked open. Standing like a monument in the middle of the dam was an old BMX bike with a few metres of rope attached to the front of it, half its wheel buried in the earth. When Sammy and him were young they used to ride that bike off the jetty his father had made for them, flipping themselves into the water, jumping clear before the bike slapped into the dam top. That was the last summer they had with Sam before they lost him when a tractor rolled. He remembers the blood on the wheat.

Jack closes his eyes and tries to shake the memory from his mind.

He walks around the perimeter and sees the remains of a large cow, her dead calf by her side. The skin covers the bones like a hastily arranged shelter, the skeleton bleached white. *They have been here a while,* Jack thought.

With the sun finally beginning to show itself, Jack jumps aboard his bike and guns it for home. There were two hundred head of cattle in this paddock alone when he checked online last week, and now there's nothing but bones and skeletons.

When Jack arrives home his father is having a coffee and smoking a cigarette on the front verandah.

When did he start that rubbish?

His father looked down at him as he cut the engine.

'Shall we finish what we started, here? That trailer isn't going to fix itself.'

Finished, they pull the box trailer into the large machinery shed by the house. The door shudders and creaks and the heavy chains pool noisily as its mouth opens. His father has a look of wonder smeared over his face and Jack thinks to himself that the pressure has finally got to him. The block of sunlight on the concrete floor grows until it hits something and is thrown back into their faces. Jack is blinded by the intensity. His dad is bathed in a golden glow. An old FJ Holden immaculately restored sits there grinning like a wag.

'What's this, then?' Jack said, his brow like a road map.

'It's for you, ya dill.'

'What? Why?'

'Well, we can't have you towing this beautiful box trailer behind that heap,' he said, using his head to motion towards the saggy, powder blue HQ behind them, his face cracked open by the broadest smile Jack had seen on him in years.

'But how did you pay for it?'

'How do you think?' he said, as the two men inched towards the gleaming beast, tentative, as though if they moved too fast they would startle it and it would bolt off, out into the dry.

Reclining Monk – *Kokkai Ng*

Catullus XIII

Translated by Thomas Gardner

You'll eat well at my place, Fabullus,
If you're lucky, and you bring plenty of pizza
And a hot babe and some goon and a good mood.
It's BYO so if you bring all this it should be chill.
Sorry, I'm piss-poor at the moment.
But in return I can give you some aftershave
Some Venus chick gave to my missus.
When you smell that shit,
You'll want to be a fucking nose.

Offcuts

Kelli Lonergan

'So how long have you been a vego for?' Gus asked, mouth full of lamb kofta and fork horizontally raised as a kind of mini baton to indicate exactly whose turn it was to speak.

Not that there would be any confusion. Forty minutes into the dinner party and Jenna was the only one whose seat at the table was systematically bypassed as the succession of meat-based dishes made their way around to the other guests' plates. As a pity prize, she had been permitted to keep at her permanent disposal, the half-filled bowls of hummus and tabouli that had already been picked over as entrees.

'Why didn't you tell them I don't eat meat?' Jenna hissed at Will. It was early in the evening and they had been ushered outside with the other guests as they stood around the garden, sipping glasses of wine. It was also the third time since arriving, that Jenna had been forced to politely decline Gus's offer of kebabs.

'You forgot to remind me,' said Will, right hand clutching at his collection of skewers. 'Where do you think I'm supposed to put these?'

Jenna couldn't argue. In the past she was always the one who accepted the invitations for dinner parties, casually calling a few days in advance to apologetically inform the hosts of her non-carnivorous diet. Usually, it was never a problem. However, they were now dining at the house of Will's boss and Jenna had failed to take into account her partner's hopelessness when it came to remembering the limitations of her eating habits.

'You eat chicken don't you?' Gus said, tongs in hand.

'No sorry, I don't eat chicken either. Thank you though.'

'Come on, a little chicken isn't going to kill you.'

Jenna forced a polite smile. 'That's okay, really. I'm fine with the dips.'

Gus scoffed and turned to Will, 'Women and their bloody diets. She looks like she could do with a bit of meat. Some stamina for later, hey?' He elbowed Will, as if prompting the expected chauvinistic chuckle before moving on to barrage the next couple with another set of inappropriate jokes.

'What's his problem?'

Will put his arm around Jenna and drew her to his chest. 'Sorry, he's just one of those guys who love their barbeque.'

Jenna buried a snigger into Will's shirt.

'At least the wine is good,' offered Will.

The brute had cracked out his best semillon for the occasion. One of the perks of accepting dodgy money from the local foresting company, Jenna guessed. When Will had taken the job at the city's rag, she had been the first to remind him of the paper's dubious political omissions concerning the new pulp mill.

'What about your dream of becoming the next Woodward?' Jenna had said when they first discussed the topic.

'Just think of it this way,' said Will as he prepared that evening's dinner.

'I'll be closer to the inside scandal than Woodward ever was.'

'Yeah well, Woodward didn't work for Nixon,' Jenna had muttered, her words muted by the violent sound of Will's chopping.

Looking around the party now, she doubted any of the other employees had even heard of Woodward. She recognised one of the columnists, a fifty-year-old bottle-blonde whose picture, smiling smugly out of the folds of the paper, never failed to induce a sudden onset of nausea. Her column was devoted entirely to recounting the mundane details of her family. It was as if she were one of those acquaintances who, every time you ran into one another, would update you on the mind-numbing trivialities of children who you had never even met.

'Alright everyone, let's move inside for the grand-ay spread,' Gus bellowed across the yard, bringing them to this point in time and the aforementioned 'Vegetarian question'.

'It's gotta be some kind of diet thing, right?' said Gus, without even waiting for Jenna's answer.

The columnist quickly piped in. 'But if you were starving and there was nothing else, you would eat meat right?' She looked at Jenna and smirked. 'Don't tell me that if you were stuck in the wilderness you wouldn't kill an animal to survive.'

If I were stuck in the wilderness with you, the animal wouldn't be the first to go, thought Jenna. 'It's just a preference really. I have nothing against people who eat meat,' said Jenna, hoping to bring the conversation to an end.

'Well, I certainly didn't fight my way to the top of the food chain to eat salad,' said Gus, bearing his teeth like a starved Rottweiler. 'These choppers were made for steak.'

Under the table, Will squeezed Jenna's hand. She secretly wished he would stand up for her but didn't blame him for not getting involved.

'Well I hope you've all saved room for the pièce de résistance,' said Gus, standing up.

'There's more?' Jenna whispered to Will. He shrugged his shoulders and looked at her apologetically. She got the feeling that the dinner would not end until Gus had successfully afflicted everyone with coronaries.

'Here we go folks,' said Gus, re-entering the room. 'Courtesy of head office.'

A tray was presented onto the centre of the table, the charcoaled mound upon its surface popping and wheezing. It wasn't hard to guess who Gus meant by head office.

'That's the biggest fucking roast I've ever seen,' said Will.

'Not just any roast,' said Gus.

Jenna studied the engorged mass of meat on the tray. The smell of roast on a Sunday evening at Will's parents' house was the only time she ever felt slightly tempted by the idea of meat. This was different though. Amid the scent of rosemary and onion came a smell Jenna couldn't identify. It was like old dishwashing liquid mixed with burning rubber. She looked around to see if anyone else noticed. If they did they certainly weren't showing it.

'This here, my friends,' said Gus, running his carving knife across the sharpening rod, 'is what they call a Turducken.'

'I've heard of these,' said Will aloud. 'There's a duck stuffed in there too right?'

Jenna felt her stomach turn.

Gus laughed. 'Rookie mistake, William. There isn't just a duck stuffed in here.'

The roast, fresh from the barbeque, would not stop hissing. From its sides, blisters of fat popped like bubble wrap and the whole thing seemed to tremble with heat.

'The Turducken,' continued Gus, 'is a turkey, stuffed with a duck that is stuffed with a chicken.' Jenna winced at each emphatic proclamation of the word, 'stuffed'.

'Like a babushka of fowl,' said Will, clearly pleased with himself for coming up with the analogy. 'Why eat one when you can eat them all in one *fowl* swoop?'

The whole table laughed except for Jenna. She noticed that the roast was not trembling but shaking, the sides of the turkey rising. The stream of liquid that had leaked around the tray was yellow and streaked with what looked like black phlegm.

'For that one, Rookie, you get the honours of carving.'

Grinning, Will stood up and took the knife from Gus. If Jenna wasn't so busy watching the roast she would have been annoyed at her husband's new found affiliation.

The noise was the first thing that everyone noticed. It was as if someone had burst a balloon right in Jenna's ear. A balloon filled with the sour stench of month-old potato salad. Jenna could hear the other guests' cries of disgust through the cloud of reeking fumes that had fogged up the length of the table. The columnist was the first one to scream.

'What the fuck?' shouted Gus. A plate shattered and as everyone hurried to move away, the legs of chairs scraped the ground.

'Somebody get it,' yelled Will and it was then that Jenna could see what he was referring to.

It was unlike anything she had seen before, perhaps because its feathers were missing. It was running blindly across the tabletop, its body half-decayed, the other half, raw and mottled pink.

'Get it with your fork,' someone shouted to the columnist as it ran to the side where she was standing.

'I can't,' she shrieked, waving the utensil before her.

Jenna was the only one who was still sitting at the table. As it came towards her, its beak agape and its black eyes flared, she didn't once think of moving.

'Jesus Christ.' Jenna felt Will at her side but saw only the flash of the skewer as the wooden point pinned it down, the face upon the twisted neck caught somewhere between fear and resignation.

Later it would become known that the fumes emitted from the pulp mill had been infecting the livestock on a nearby farm. However, no mention of the incident was ever made, other than in the columnist's brief piece towards the end of the paper titled, 'Vegetarian Nearly Killed by a Little Chicken'.

Florence's Valentine

Celeste Moore

i buried myself
inside the echo of
the shallow beating heat
in your cavernous chest

the rhythm is a beat
i can't get out
i tap it on plastic tables
in fast food joints
on subways
through the 3am pub haze
my sneakers
tread lightly on
the pavement of
your backbone

i'll meet you where
your spine ends.

The Courtesan's Version

Claire Hansen

This isn't really how it happened. The heroine of the tale doesn't typically become a fluttering, feathery courtesan, least of all an unsuccessful one, eventually reduced to walking the streets, from alehouse to alehouse, lifting her skirts for coin. Nor does the prophesied boy-king, my would-be saviour, end up hauling horse dung from dawn to dusk, nought but a stable boy.

This isn't where it should start, either, after the end of the tale; and a miserable, anticlimactic end it makes too. No wordsmith worth his salt would deign to tell our tale, halting and feeble as it is. So I will tell it, seeing as I can't be the heroine anymore, and all the poets are dead.

Everyone had heard of the prophecy, of the orphan boy who would come from the south, burning bright with supernaturally sanctioned right to sweep in and save us from the invaders. The prophets sang songs of him, and published stories of his exploits. The tales trickled from the highest tower to the grubbiest shack in the City, and people ate the stories up like the words would fill their stomachs, and then they repeated and regurgitated the stories until fact and fable were so incestuously interbred that the tale reproduced itself into a self-spinning, monstrous, malformed entity beyond anyone's control.

The basic ingredients were memorable enough, as I know them. The prophesied boy-king was one of our own, a scrubby, short, country-born, dark-haired boy of no notable family, not one of the tall proud invaders who had installed themselves in the palace after the trickling out of the old line. The invaders had come from the north, bringing – at first – aid and comfort during the last of the famines. Our people welcomed them openly, naively, as friends. I remembered the tales about these folk from my childhood, blonde-haired saviours from the strange and rich northern lands. They brought new fruits and untasted flavours, full coffers and rich, gleaming furs stripped from the wild backs of creatures exotic and unheard of. I do not remember when they turned against us, or even how. It was as if we awoke one day to find them closing the doors of the palaces and great houses against us, homes we would only re-enter through the service gates. About this time the old legends of the boy-king began to be retold. Sometimes they would catch the tellers and string them up like bloody party lanterns across the bridge, carrion warnings of the danger of our stories. But the blood of the writers fed the tales like their inks never could, giving visceral truth to misty legend. The old prophets that sometimes visited the innermost bowels of the City, its musty smoky taverns and theatres, brothels and bear pits, would tell new visions of the future, and news of the present, leaked from the untamed southern lands, of a famous old mystic and his protégé, an orphan child raised from dirt who would one day pull the carpet from the pale unworked feet of our new tyrants. It was said he rode with dragons and was visited by visions, he could fight like the devil and his thoughts could move mountains. The gods had kissed his brow, the prophets said.

They call him Prince, now, for the other stable boys like to crown him with horse dung after a long day's shovelling. I always wondered why the northerners didn't string his body up too, but the other girls had heard it from their local patrons that it just goes to show how powerless he is, that they didn't even need to cut his throat. Most folk still knew him as *that* boy, the disappointment who thought he could oust the northerners. I never paid much attention to this so-called Prince or his dung-throwing followers – unless, of course, they had the coin to see me through the rent – until I noticed Prince one sweltering summer's afternoon, resting against a sack of dung bound for the lower gardens. His forgettable face, summered brown and sheened with sweat, had a coat of pain about it that day. His thin, lanky body – the one folk said was made for coronet, armour, and glory – looked worn out, its best days long behind it. He was no longer a boy, but he was nothing more than one to most.

'I have no coin for you,' he said immediately, 'and if I did I wouldn't spend it catching my death.' I shrugged and sat beside him, pulling off my sweat-stained slippers, once made for dancing and stepping lightly from carriage to dining hall, and stretching my red, swollen feet out in front of me. 'You smell like dung.' I said, wrinkling my nose. 'And hay.'

'You don't smell much better yourself. Run out of rose oil, have we?' He retorted, pulling his hat down over his eyes.

'You were supposed to save me.' I added, with no disappointment, just disinterested observation. The hat came off abruptly, and he stared at me, waiting for reproach or mockery. I shrugged. 'S'okay.' I said generously. 'Not your fault. The stories were wrong, that's all.' I wasn't sure whether he was going to yell his frustrated disappointments back at me or simply pick up his bag of manure and walk away, but in the end he did neither.

'Drink?' He asked. I nodded.

The Starving Poet was one of the few taverns in the lower City that the northerners' men did not frequent. They stayed away not because it housed subversive revolutionaries pounding beer-soaked benches and declaring their vision of the new world, but simply because it stank to high heaven, being the local watering hole for the stable boys, the tanners, and the waste-men. That, and there were pervasive tales that every housewife, whore and princess knew, tales that said the Starving Poet was haunted by the verbose ghosts of hanged writers. The ale wasn't particularly good, either, but that was neither here nor there.

I'd always found the Starving Poet a welcome refuge for the street girls, with many a stinky fellow there happy to spend his new coin on a tumble in the hay. The tavern's owner had looked a little suspiciously at Prince, but it was a quiet working afternoon, and none of his patrons seemed oppositional enough to bother kicking up a fuss about drinking with the failed hope of the south.

'I heard that the dragons are all dead.' Prince said to his cup, which he held tightly in both hands. Talking wasn't something I was used to, at that time, for it inevitably brought trouble to your door. I looked, around, nervously. Mentioning dragons or prophecies was a good way to get a short and sharp trip to the bridge.

'People will say anything. Stories are all just nonsense; you of all people should know that.' A hunched over old man perched on a barstool nearby laughed loudly at this. Prince said nothing, although his cheeks turned a darker shade of dirt. 'That's no answer,' he grumbled. 'If you don't believe they're gone, then what happened to them?'

Prince knew the stories just as well as I did, probably better, given everyone blamed him for the mass exodus of the dragons and everything like them. With the foiling of the fairytale, it was said, some of the plates in the earth shifted, and the dragons fled into the clouds, leaving no trace but old scars on the land and embroidered memories in the minds of the old.

'All I know is what people said after you … I mean, after it all went wrong. I was just a kid, like you, I just remember shadows that felt like they had no end pass over us. My pa said you could feel the difference when the dragons disappeared, like the night got a bit less black, and day got a bit less shiny.' I shrugged and signalled for another round. 'But then folks stopped getting burned up and eaten, too, so it wasn't all bad. Some people say they're not dead, just gone from these parts, along with the green folk and all the other weird creatures. Probably went to the lands the northerners left, I reckon.'

Prince, the boy-king-that-wasn't, looked ever so slightly heartened by the news. Here I was telling the same silly stories to the same silly boy whose stories got us into this mess. 'But like I said, you can't trust what people say,' I added, just to be clear. 'They're all just stories that aren't true.'

The eavesdropping old man laughed again ever so loudly now, but before I could turn around and tell him what for he had jumped nimbly off his barstool and pushed his way between us. 'Got a bone to pick with you, boy,' the man grumbled, wiping his bearded mouth with one hand and shaking an old dried-up quill in Prince's face with the other. 'Here I was churning out the great and glorious deeds you would perform, with the whole of the City lapping it up while I dodged the northerners so I didn't end up decorating their bridges with my bones … and then *you* go and get performance anxiety and let everyone down. Lost all my credibility in one fell swoop, you did. Now nobody will buy a word I write, and what's more, nobody even tries to string me up anymore.'

Prince stood, draining the last drop of ale, before he flung the mug forcefully to the floor, smiling grimly at the sound of it shattering. He looked at the old man, then at me. I waited as his mouth almost moved, a sound almost escaped. Instead he shrugged, and wordless, walked away.

The old man followed him, his little feet stepping daintily around the shattered mug as he shouted at the slightly rounded shoulders of the boy-king-that-never-would-be.

'The problem was, you see, *you* listened to the stories! You weren't supposed to do that. You set yourself up for a fall, see, because you thought it was all destined, that you didn't have to try. Like we'd done all the work for you by writing it down and telling it to each other. Like we created you. You came into the City looking all high and mighty on your overgrown pony, all underdog and no substance.'

The few pairs of eyes in the Starving Poet were now all trained on Prince's back. He turned to face them slowly, taking in the old prophet's words just like folk used to lap up stories of the boy-king all those years ago. 'Hey,' I said, not liking the look in Prince's eyes, 'It's not him that was wrong, it was everyone else. Everyone else and their prophecies!'

The old man turned back to me. 'It's not that the prophecies were wrong, it's just that's not all there is to it.' I was about to shoot back a warning that he'd have the northerners after all of us if he kept up this nonsense about prophecies and stories, but I realised that Prince had slipped away, the tavern-keeper was busy brushing away the mug shards, and we were just an old man and a tired courtesan, and neither of us had anything left to say.

The dung-king they named Prince never came back to the Starving Poet. The bells tolled that night for an unnamed crime, the northerners' boots thudded on the City's cobblestones, the three moons eclipsed, and folk said the graves yielded up their dead and the castle ramparts cracked under the black shadow of a dragon once more. I wouldn't know, having been especially busy that night. Apocalyptic fears tend to bring out the lust in people, and besides, one of the local boys was celebrating his impending nuptials. Anyway, the moons have many times fattened and shrivelled since then. But beneath them, eventually, rumours began to trickle through the long-dried veins of the City. Prince, it was said, had flown off on the back of the dragon, disappearing into the northern woods where the outcast, the green folk, and the failed heroes and prophets couched in despair. They said that one midsummer's eve, his topsy-turvy, bedraggled army thundered into the City, and by dawn the northerners had fled away, defeated and shamed. Nobody knew where they went; folk said perhaps wherever the dragons had returned from. They say the dung-king was crowned with a solid gold diadem, and that he wed a beautiful courtesan brought low by circumstance, but who, it was discovered, carried the blood of the old line of kings.

Some people who tell the story say that the old prophet in the Starving Poet was a disguised god, or the famed and elusive master of magics, reappearing to give his protégé one last chance. I don't think someone that important would smell of sweat and ale, but what would I know.

That is how it happened. At least, that is how I tell it.

That Lost Colour

Elisabeth Murray

Mum came in the door. 'Janice is back,' she said.

I looked up from the magazine. All I could see was that shot silk party dress.

'Well?' she said. 'Are you going to help with the parcels?'

Her hair was disordered from the bus. There were dark patches on the back of her dress.

'Mrs Ryan would like you to go out with her this evening,' she said.

I knelt down to put the potatoes away. The cupboard was a cavern of soil and starch. I thought I must look like I was trying to gas myself.

'Why would I want to go out with an old lady?' I said.

'Heather, don't be silly. I'm talking about Janice.'

The bag slipped. A whole lot of potatoes tumbled to the floor.

'Heather!' She had flour across her forehead. She was refilling the canisters. 'Will you be more careful! I don't know the matter with you. You've been acting peculiar all morning.'

'Me, peculiar?' I said. 'And how would you know, I've been at the chemist's.'

'Perhaps that's why you're acting queer. I don't know if it's good for a girl to do that kind of work, I just don't know.'

'Sometimes it's not good for a girl to be stony broke, sometimes it's not good for a girl to work.'

'What have I done that my only child has to be so bold? My *only* child?' She looked at the ceiling and her mouth twisted as though with something she'd never be able to swallow. I started picking up the potatoes. One looked like a head that had been in the grave for yonks.

'Will I telephone Mrs Ryan and tell her you'll be pleased to go?'

'Righto,' I said.

I stacked the potatoes like a house of cards and thought of shot silk taffeta.

Mrs Ryan was as plump as ever but her face looked pared away and cross-hatched with shadows. It felt like donkey's since I'd seen her, but didn't she come into the chemist's at least once a week? Well, I had no time to gossip with customers. I let her kiss me and said I was dead pleased Janice was back.

She was in the backyard, lying on a blanket in her bathing suit. Her curlers were as yellow as her hair. Her eyes were closed. I couldn't remember if she'd ever been pretty. She looked as if she'd bathed in butter. Her face was hollow and her body seemed swollen. The bathing suit was loose in places, tight in others. It was cherry-red and her lips and toes were painted the same colour and her skin looked yellower against them.

I leaned back on my elbows. My legs were brown on the tartan.

'Heather.' She took a gulp of air. Her eyes seemed bigger now her face was so hollow. 'Did you have a blast when you finished school?'

'Yes, I suppose so.'

She looked away into the zinnias. Her hair was so blonde in the late afternoon she was like a candle.

'What a bloody stupid time to get crook,' she said.

'What do you mean?' I said, then bit my cheek.

'Everyone finishing school and having such a blast.'

'It wasn't so crash hot. You know what I'm jazzed about. Going to university in the city. I just got a scholarship.'

'A scholarship.' Her mouth held the word like a clump of cream. 'Oh, gee.'

'But don't worry, I'm sure you can get one next year, specially if they feel sorry you were crook.'

'The city,' she said. 'Oh, gee.' When she looked at me I could only think of corridors, sterility like a tongue up your nose. 'Just wait 'til you see my dress. Ma made it for a welcome home present. It's super.'

'I bet,' I said. But a dress is nothing until it's on a body.

Mrs Ryan came out with tea and cake. 'Now Janice love, mind you eat up,' she said. She stood there while Janice bit into a slice of orange cake. A piece of icing stuck on her lipstick like a tooth. 'I've asked Peter Reilly if he wouldn't like to take you out tonight,' she said.

'Peter *Reilly*?' cried Janice. 'Why, Ma?'

'Because I bumped into his mother at the baker's and she said he'd be delighted to know you're back.' She spoke as though nothing could fluster her now her daughter was lying here. 'You used to find him charming love, don't pretend now.'

Janice's mouth was open. There was a sheet of cake over her tongue. Mrs Ryan went back across the lawn trilling a Christmas carol.

'Maybe I should forget about coming,' I said. 'If you're going to be with Peter.'

'Oh, no!' she said. She was scarfing cake. She swallowed. 'No, you have to, I wouldn't be seen dead alone with Peter.'

I sipped my tea. The glare dropped away and mozzies emerged from the heat. Janice lifted her leg as though to detect a tan. We took the blanket and dishes inside. Mrs Ryan was cooking chops for Mr Ryan. In the living room Janice's brothers were fighting over a train set.

Her bedroom was a sick peach colour in the electric light and seemed like a memory. Stumbling about in heels and feather boas, making cakes, putting dolls to bed. While Janice was having a bath I got out of my dress and stood in my girdle and stockings. My skin didn't have the caramel gleam anymore. My face was pasty in the pink framed mirror. I yanked on my party dress. The chiffon was cool, green as health. Janice came back in a white towel bringing a stream of soap. She was clean in the way those corridors must be.

'You look super.' She sank onto the bed. She was holding the towel at her chest and it split at her thigh like when you cut into a lemon pie.

'Put on your dress,' I said. 'I bet it's swell.'

She went behind the wardrobe door and I carried on lining my eyes. I didn't tell her she appeared in the corner of the mirror. I expected red patches, bruises, needle-holes, but there was only yellow flesh.

She stepped out in a pink dress with flowers and ribbons crammed on the bust. It stuck to her hips and finished too late.

'See?' I said. 'Knockout.'

'Will you put on my make-up? I don't want to look like an invalid.'

'Okay,' I said, though I'm no miracle worker.

I touched her face like a mortician. When she closed her eyes I felt as if I was alone in the room. Her lips parted as I drew around them. Her breath dampened my fingers. I spread on the lipstick she'd been wearing earlier. I rolled a powder puff across her mouth and dabbed it with a handkerchief. I stepped back. She smiled. It looked as if she'd put her lips in a puddle of blood. As if I'd prepared her for Halloween.

'Knockout,' I said.

She sat on the bed to take out her hair and I freshened mine up in the mirror. It didn't look like mine. It was dusty, limp. I wanted to get into the soft light of the dance hall.

'Heather, I really hope we can hang out this summer.'

'Okay,' I said. 'But I work at the chemist, remember.'

'I know,' she said. 'Just now and then. I've been cooped up for ten months.'

'Aren't you supposed to be recovering?'

She came to the mirror and sprayed her hair from a rusty can which made the room smell like someone had tried to rid it of cockroaches. She yanked a handkerchief out of her bust and hawked into it. I thought I saw red flecks scatter airborne.

'I feel right as rain,' she said.

I put on some perfume I got for Christmas. I knew my mother had saved for months. There was a grim look on my father's face and he muttered, 'Well, we've only got one kid, I s'pose you have to spoil her.' Normally my mother would have wept or dropped something or gone into the bedroom but I was smiling so brilliantly he was like a radio in the next room. The bottle was warm and had a woman's curves. The fragrance made me think of the lingerie a real lady wears, over clean powdered skin. But this room made it cold and musty on my skin.

The kitchen light was the deep yellow that comes near evening. A serial was playing on the radio. Mr Ryan was eating his tea at the table, one hand wrapped around a bottle of Foster's. Janice's brothers went back to their trains. Dirt was engraved in their toenails. Mrs Ryan sat at the table trying to restrain the baby in her lap. Little Danny squirmed in his chair. Honking sounded from outside.

'That's Robert,' I said.

'Maybe Peter brought him along for you,' said Janice. 'So you won't feel cut out.'

I held my tongue. Mrs Ryan followed us into the hall. The baby twisted in her arms.

'I want you to put your stole on now love,' she said.

Peter wore a grey suit with a handkerchief falling out of the pocket. He had dust-coloured hair and sunburn across his nose. Behind him was Robert's Cadillac, green in the house light.

'Peter, take care of my little girl, won't you?'

He shifted his weight. We heard Danny fussing and Mr Ryan getting mad. 'Certainly I will, ma'am.'

I went down the steps. I heard Mrs Ryan say, 'I wouldn't guess you even suffered a cold, love.'

Robert was holding the door and my heels were clicking on the road and in the minute before night my dress was green as jewels.

'Jazzed to have you back, Janice,' said Robert when she and Peter climbed into the back seat.

'Yeah, jazzed,' said Peter. He'd watch Janice for a bit then turn to the window. She was sitting with her hands in her lap. She could have been a little girl or an old lady.

Robert winked at me. I raised my eyebrows. The houses were lit like daisies and men were coming home from work or the pub and children were ploughing on with their cricket games and people were sitting on their porches.

Robert parked near the dance hall and reached beneath his seat and took a swig from a paper bag. His mouth stiffened and he wiped it with the back of his hand and passed it to me. It was harsh and dirty. Robert laughed. I raised my eyebrows. I passed it to Peter who took it as if it was a dead possum.

'What about me?' said Janice. Peter looked at her. 'I'm Gonna Knock on Your Door' came on. After the whisky I liked it better than usual. I wanted to get into the hall.

'But Janice, do you reckon you ought to?'

'Why d'you have to be such a wet rag, Peter?'

He handed it to her. She swallowed as though it was gravel. On the radio Eddie was telling his girl he was gonna knock and ring and tap until she came out. Robert took another mouthful and stowed it away. He jumped out and came around to my door. Janice was halfway out, reaching for Peter, when she doubled over and shuddered as though a live thing was caught inside her. She let Peter help her out. He didn't step back. She was pressed against him.

'I shouldn't've given you that whisky,' he said.

Robert took my elbow and headed for the hall. People leaned on the bonnets of cars smoking. There was a quick tune coming across the lot.

I had the same good feeling I had every Saturday though I knew it wasn't anything special. There was a band that'd been here a hundred times; four fellows wearing white suits and pink grins. The same table with the purple tablecloth and the punch and sandwiches against the back wall. The same crowd eating or dancing or gassing.

'This is swell!' said Janice. The whisky had put colour on her cheeks. 'Let's go dance.'

'You ought to take it easy,' said Peter.

'I'm going to find a boy to dance with,' she said.

'Oh – no, all right.' He trailed her to the floor.

The band started up a slow tune. Robert took my hand. It felt like my father leading me to bed.

'What do you think about Janice?' I said.

'What d'you mean what do I think about her?' His face looked like an assortment of separate parts.

'Never mind,' I said.

The band began a sunnier song. He seized my waist and span me. The whisky fizzed in my throat. Goodbye cruel world, I'm off to join the circus. He swung me away and then close. My skirt caught the air full and green and rustling like luxury. My breath was heavy. I felt my body as only dancing can make you feel it. So shut inside your body and yet so free in it. The swing of my body like the swoop of the band like the rush of my breath. Paint my face with a good-for-nothing smile, 'cause a mean fickle woman turned my whole world upside down. His hair was like Coca-Cola with the light through it. What if we never stopped, what if we whirled on through time so we never slowed?

Then Janice was asking me to come to the loo. I felt my heart slowing as though all along it had been waiting to get back its old rhythm.

'I'm gonna dance with Patty Kelly,' called Robert. 'Better get ya skates on.'

The ladies' room was strawberry-coloured with a vase of dead flowers on the sink. Margie O'Doherty and Pam Wilkinson were pinned to the mirror putting on lipstick. They didn't notice us. When Janice came out of the loo I heard Margie cry, 'Oh, g'day Janice! We heard you were back from beyond.'

I made for the sink farthest from Janice.

'Oh, Heather, your dress! I wish I had your figure.'

'You look terrific Margie. And Pam, that frock is swell!'

They laughed with their crimson mouths and patted the undersides of their hair. 'Well, we'll be missed,' Margie said and they bugged out.

Janice started powdering her face. In the hard light it looked as if she was dabbing on chalk. I looked at my reflection. I'd put on too much mascara. I looked like a burlesque woman.

'Gee Robert's a swell dancer,' she said.

'Wanta dance with him?'

She looked at me. 'Bet you wouldn't hand him over to Margie that fast.'

I wanted to tell her she should just take what she could get with Peter but I heard myself say, 'Why not? He's just a boy.'

She was staring. 'You mean … You don't – Oh God, I don't see why I should spend a lifetime in the sanatorium and when I get out I should have a bloody rotten time.' She dropped into a wicker chair.

All the spirit from dancing was gone. What did it matter if I spent the rest of the night in here and Robert danced with Patty Kelly and every other scag?

'What was the place like, Janice?'

She started dragging her nails on the wicker. 'Oh, peaceful. Would you believe there's somewhere more peaceful than this place?' She looked at me. 'I didn't see anything. I just sat and listened to the ladies yabbering and choking for breath.' She stopped the scratching. 'So you're scooting off to the city. What in the world am I going to do?'

I saw the city floating above this place, ripped free out of sheer energy … It'd be better than dancing, I'd be shot through with light and my heart would go like a drill.

She pulled her foot onto her knee. I saw the tops of her stockings. She kneaded her ankle.

'Maybe Robert should take you home,' I said. 'You don't look so well.'

'Oh, gee whiz!' She got up and went out.

Two girls from the fourth form came in. They were laughing, their faces open and pink. They stopped when they saw me. I went out feeling like a schoolmistress.

The floor was jumping with lurid dresses and dull suits. Everything was so loud, everyone so close, the sax ruptured through the words of 'Boom Boom Baby', a fellow rammed into me and only grinned as though we were both dancing as crazy as each other. I called out to Robert but I couldn't hear my voice.

Then he was at my elbow with that crazy smile saying, 'It had the beat that she liked best, I couldn't stop her and you know the rest.' We danced through all the numbers and I was waiting for that feeling. But when people started to drift to the punch and chairs and then to the doors and the band eased off I just felt relieved.

'We better find Pete and Janno,' he said.

'We'll never find them in here.' I caught his hand and made a beeline for the doors.

The night smelled of smokes and sweat. Margie and Pam were going down the steps with the Connolly boys.

'Robbie Sullivan,' Alan Dodd called. 'Come along to the park, we got beer and Bev Kennedy.'

'Not tonight mate,' said Robert. 'I got whisky and a girl of my own.'

We lit smokes in the car. 'One Last Kiss' was playing, the loneliest song in the world. Robert put his arm across my shoulder.

'Another drink?' I said.

He reached under the seat, took a swallow and held it where I couldn't reach it. 'I don't want you getting canned tonight, baby.' He laughed and handed it over.

My mouth shrivelled as if it was moonshine. I saw Janice and Peter coming through the glassy lines of cars. She was carrying her stole and her shoulders were so bright it looked like a trick of the moon. As she slid across the seat her knickers winked at the top of her thighs. Robert's mouth was open. He took the whisky from me and handed it to Peter.

'Take a big slug, bud.'

As Peter swallowed his eyes bugged the same colour as the whisky. When Janice reached out he let her have it.

Robert started the engine. 'Where to, folks?' he said.

'Oughtn't we take Janice home?' said Peter. His voice was a little loose.

'Will you cut it out?' said Janice. She took another swig.

'I don't think you ought to do that.'

'Don't you?' She tipped her head back and her throat swelled white.

'Peter was hired by your mother,' laughed Robert. 'And he wants his dough.'

When we got on the road the noise of the dance fell away. The red dirt is a better barricade than prison or hospital walls. A jazz tune coiled out of the radio like the smoke from my mouth. The lawns were lighter than the night, neat as carpet. The chrome in driveways was the only shining thing.

We came to the lot owned by Old Crone Maguire until her husband died and she was carted off to the asylum. Now there's only busted cars. The grass has been gnawed away by oil. It looks like a place once covered by sea, prehistoric carcasses exposed. There is a graveyard overlooking a drop.

'What's the matter honey doll?' said Robert.

'Why'd you bring us here?' My breath came out in smoke.

He laughed. 'It's a beaut view.' He got out and peered in the back window. 'Will the Archduke and his mistress be getting out?'

Peter fumbled with the door and stood blinking at the dark waste. Janice gripped his arm as though she might fall and break.

'So long!' said Robert. He took my hand and we started off, keeping the same distance from the graves as though there was a field of electricity. I could make out Janice by the flash of her dress and the glow of her hair but she could have been a foot or a mile away.

The backs of my legs smacked into a bumper guard and I thought I was winded but he was breathing over my mouth and our breath was mingling, whisky-sweet. The bonnet was hard in the small of my back and the grill burned my calves. I wanted his whole weight on me. To feel every inch of my own skin and nerves. I wanted nothing between us, but wasn't it impossible?

'Don't rumple my skirt, sir.'

He straightened up and watched me. Then he laughed.

'I love you and I want to get hitched,' he said.

'Okay, Rock Hudson.'

He put a cigarette between my lips and lit it. He lit one for himself.

'What you looking for?' he said.

I tapped off the ash. 'Those folks we came with.'

'Oh, they're around somewhere.'

'Dead romantic spot,' I said.

The glow of my cigarette moved through the dark a foot from his, like two planets in the same orbit. His face was lit as he pulled on it, then obscured by smoke.

I was listening to the blur the whisky made in my head and when the noise started it was like smoke creeping under a door. It sounded like a baby animal trapped in the roof. My heels were slipping in the earth and Robert was holding me. We were going towards the graves.

'I'll go look for them,' he said. 'You wait here.'

'Don't be a mug.' I tugged him closer.

He laughed. 'That's right, can't leave you to be roughed up by ghosts.'

I pulled him through the gravestones. How could her weeping have carried so far? The dark seemed as dense as the ocean.

She was sitting on a grave cover, her dress trailing in the soil. Her suspenders and an inch of her thigh were showing. Peter was perched at her feet trying to keep his trousers off the dirt. He was looking at her as at a painting that seemed obscene but in a way he couldn't put his finger on. He jumped up when he saw us.

'I don't know – she just started crying!'

I went around the grave and my heel clipped the corner and I saw myself plummeting to the pink-roofed houses with carports and hedges and children in animal print pyjamas and women with dyed hair curled inside men with fuzzy paunches.

'Trust me mate,' said Robert. 'You don't want to get caught in a mess like this.'

'What mess?' said Peter.

I sat next to Janice. The stone was still warm from the day.

'What's buzzin'?' I said. I could see the whisky in her eyes but they were so wet and blue there had to be something else.

'Why don't you mugs go and have another drink of lunatic soup?' I said.

'That stuff cost me a fortune,' said Robert. 'I want to put it to good use, don't I?' But after a moment he went off. Peter took a squiz at me, Janice, and me again and finally beetled off. Sooner than I expected I heard the car door open and blurred voices. The moon was small on the dirt and gave no hint about the distance.

I hated the sound of her crying. I wanted to hightail it back to Robert. This place was like sorrow made into landscape. Something moved behind me. There was just a car with no wheels slumped in the dirt but something had me jittery. Old Crone Maguire's husband, coming through a place he never owned. Maybe Old Crone Maguire had carked it in the asylum and come back resentful. Jimmy, still little ... Wasn't this the place where he disappeared? It may as well have been. Janice was with us that day. We were supposed to be minding him and now he was dark, quiet, always little. I wanted to think she knew something after being where she had for ten months, but she was here now, as bound in her body as I was in mine. Everything else was vague, quiet, the place where everything lost went, all around us but impossible to reach. I don't know if I moved towards her or she moved towards me but her mouth was slack as cloth and mine cut through to her teeth and everything was wet so I thought this might be a body half rotted by rain. I recoiled. I put my wrist to my face but the perfume had worn off. I stood up.

'C'mon, let's split.'

She got up like a candle flaring in a breeze. Her dress seemed cut lower; the line at her chest was steep as the drop.

Robert drove with one hand on my leg. The earth at the edge of the road was blood dried dark. Janice's head was on Peter's chest. He smoked with his chin high and blew over her hair so it grew the same colour as his eyes. That vague quiet lost colour.

We stopped outside a white house with blue awnings. 'So long mate,' said Robert.

'I think I oughta take Janice,' said Peter.

'It's okay,' I said. 'We live close, I'll get her home.'

'No, I'm gonna take her,' said Peter. 'She can't go home like this.' He lifted her head off him, opened the door and jogged around the car. He grabbed her hand and she climbed out like a child being led up to bed.

Robert pulled away. They became a ludicrous couple in the wing mirror, him scrawny in the shapeless suit, smoking like a toff, her pink as a bridesmaid and blitzed as a sailor. I watched until I couldn't anymore. The car stopped outside Mrs Byrne's.

'Drive on, James,' I said.

He laughed and leaned over me. I kept him there a while. When I moved to get out he held my arm.

'I saved the bottom of the bottle for you.'

'Damn you,' I said.

He laughed. 'I never knew whisky made you mean,' he said. He took off the lid. That downhearted croon about the little boy lost came on the radio. But there's danger in this country that man has seldom crossed. Robert jabbed it off. He looked at the dark dirty bottle. I wanted him to grab my jaw and pour it down my throat. The car drifted to my house.

'Night, Nell.'

'Night, Mr Shawnessy.'

The night smelled of trampled roses. I heard the car snarl away down the road. Before I could get to the door it swung in. Mum stood there in her nightdress and curlers. There was no light in the house and a faraway streetlight rumpled her face. She took me in her arms.

'My little girl. Oh, I should never let my children out of my sight. Oh Lord, thank you.'

As I went along the hall I wondered if she'd noticed I was coloured different. I didn't turn on my bedroom light. I let my dress drop to the floor. When I took out my earrings a whole lot of blood came with them and I sat pushing my hanky to my ears and listening to the night which had never seemed louder or foggier.

Robert was walking me home from the chemist's a couple of days later when someone called my name from behind a cypress hedge. Janice sat in a wicker chair on her veranda in a brown shirtwaist. She had a magazine and a cup of tea.

'Did you get home in the end the other night?' I said.

Her eyes went all over me as though she was trying to place me.

'I'm getting married,' she said.

'What!' I looked at Robert. He stood there with his hands in his pockets.

Janice drank her tea. Her face was yellow against the china.

'Married to who?' I said.

'Oh, Peter Reilly of course!' She gave a laugh.

'But – Did something happen?'

'Yes, he asked me to marry him.' She started coughing, her tongue in her bottom lip, her face colouring.

When she recovered Robert strode forward and kissed her cheek. 'Congratulations Janey, I saw Pete the other day, he was on cloud nine.'

'Oh, congratulations.' I pecked her cheek. It was cold and dry.

Robert leaned against the porch post and lit a smoke. Birds cawed, coming in for the evening.

'Well, I gotta blow,' he said. He put a kiss on my cheek. He was going down the steps and there was nothing I could say to stop him.

'Heather, you left your things here,' said Janice.

She struggled out of the chair. The magazine smacked on the ground. I picked it up. A garble of cakes and dresses and advertisements for soap. The sounds of a baby crying and boys bickering came through the house. Janice returned with a paper bag. It was my makeup and the blue dress. Knickknacks I'd left here years ago. I wondered if she'd ask me to have a cup of tea.

'I'd better go,' I said gesturing at the sky. She nodded and gave a smile. I went down the steps. On the last I turned and said, 'I'm glad you're home.'

I couldn't tell if she still had the smile on. The porch was all wrong in the lowering sun. The dress made her hips look very wide.

'You know, if you need something … well, I work at the chemists … you don't have to …' I felt like a kid trying to tell a story they knew their mother knew was a lie.

'I thought I saw Jimmy in the … where I was,' she said.

My heart vaulted to my throat. The sun had moved. She was the pigtailed girl in beads and a feather boa.

'I'm glad you're home,' I said. I was on the footpath. I heard the creak of the wicker and the scratch of the magazine and when I started home all I saw was the white cornice and the cypress hedge.

(k)new wor(l)d

Claire Hansen

The scent of the unknown hits, rudely, square
In the face, words permeating the air.
Rushing out, the keen disciplining tide
Of words circumvented, unread, untried.

Branded in the thin woody flesh, bright shades
Of red and black, forbidding dates displayed.
The history of its travels inked within,
A record of births – where past lives begin.

And hidden in its pages, fugitives of lead,
Illicit footprints, the words of the dead.
Long-gone explorers mark this little world;
In musty depths long-since they trawled and pearled.

(k)new wor(l)d

Bled for ink and netted for its treasures,
Delphic worlds unveiled, their auguries measured.
Taking what we need, in quotes, line or verse,
Retired hunters no longer traverse

Its yellowing lands. We silence its story,
We close its mouth, taking our quest's glory:
Our only trophy, poached of its body –
To be reborn, and elsewhere embodied.

The Flash

Harriet Westcott

Button

It started, as these things often do, out of boredom and by accident. I was at work. I input data. I sat at my computer, which in turn sat on my small brown-coloured desk. My computer is old, and it takes a bit of time to save. Often I would have to wait for some seconds, after inputting a batch of numbers, before I could continue. On that particular day for some reason, during that barely perceptible pause after pressing control-save, I looked up to the only other person I share an office with. A man. He was new when it happened, and we had only been in the same room for about a week. I couldn't remember his name. He was looking at me with a certain regard, an expression I cannot define. He seemed immobile, and slightly drawn forward. This gaze of his was sufficient to stir something in me, however, which led me to follow the direction of his eyes to their conclusion at my sternum. The button of my blouse was undone. I was hunched over slightly and this made the fabric on either side of my shirt gape in a sort of raindrop shape, revealing a small section of my bra. It wasn't a nice one either, a bit old, a bit grey from being in the washing machine with darker coloured clothes when the dye has run.

I'm not sure why, but instead of quickly doing up the button, which is what I would like to tell you I did, or at least, what you might expect, I sat back in my chair. Looking at him I reclined and undid another button, between my nipples, pushing my shoulders back to make the fabric open wider to show the space between my breasts. All the while I watched him. He quickly looked away, and resumed his tap tapping at the keyboard. Perhaps he turned a little pink, although I cannot be sure. The room is quite gloomy and accentuates shadows, especially in the winter afternoons. By the time I went back to my work and this long minute had passed, I was a changed person.

That night I went home, as I always do, to my studio flat and fed my white cat Furry some tuna. My own dinner was eaten perched on my bed while watching television. After the meal I went to the window as I sometimes do and watered the potted plants on the ledge, picking off the dead leaves, throwing them outside into the night. I watched the darkness of the sky and the outline of other peoples' roofs. The city hummed. I made myself a cup of peppermint tea. By nine-thirty I was under the covers, light out by ten, with Furry asleep on my toes. This routine I continued: get up, go to work, go home, feed cat, (water plants), sleep, for over a week without thinking any more about my button.

One morning as I was getting up, I looked at that bra – the old grey one – sitting on top of a pile of clothes that were folded on a chair next to my bed. I picked it up and threw it in the bin. I didn't want to go to work that day, so I called in sick. Feeling perfectly fine, better than fine, in fact, almost ecstatic, I bounded out of my studio flat, down the stairs to the bottom of my building, and out the front door. It slammed loudly behind me. I got on a bus, taking it all the way to Oxford Street, where I got off outside an underwear shop.

I have never been one for fuss or pretty things. My underwear is functional, it keeps things warm, and in the right place. That is about it. I'm a practical sort of a person, neat, and thorough, not given to whimsy. I was surprised then by how exciting the fabrics around me were to look at. I darted about, not sure whether to start with paisley, or leopard, or lace. I touched the materials, feeling soft, and satiny, cool against my fingers. I grabbed bundles of bras, then corsets, panties and shorts, and camisoles with shoestring straps. I ventured into the changing room and tried them all on. By the time I emerged from the shop it was past lunchtime. I was extremely hungry and had made several purchases. I walked slowly home, enjoying the faint afternoon sunshine. Once inside I took off all my clothes and put on a new bra, and lay on my bed for a very long time. I forgot to feed Furry. At dusk I got up, and retrieved the old bra from the bin. It was slightly brown-stained on one side from where it had rested on a wet used teabag. I addressed an envelope, put the bra inside and stuffed it in my handbag. I just needed to buy a stamp, write on the name, and it was ready to post. It was Wednesday, and I resolved to take the rest of the week off.

Tube

I travel by train to work. The Monday after I bought my new bras, I got on the tube as usual and sat down without looking at anyone. I rested my arms on the handbag propped on top of my knees, and waited. By the third stop the train was quite full and people were standing. Even though it was still winter the atmosphere was stuffy, and people were sweating beneath too many layers of clothing. A tallish, thin looking gentleman, with glasses and a balding pate was swaying above me and to my left, clinging on to the rail with a look of grim nonchalance as the train braked and accelerated its way along the tunnel. I could see his reflection in the blackness of the window.

Swaying my left hand around as if I was limply conducting a small orchestra in the carriage, I got his attention. I slowly reached in towards my neck, inclining my head slightly backwards, allowing my hair to slip behind my shoulder, and played with my collar. Just between my thumb and index finger, a gentle tugging. Maintaining the impression of absent-mindedness, I ran my fingers along my collarbone and towards the buttons, which I then undid. First one, then another, and then another, until the purple of my newly purchased bra became visible beneath my black cotton shirt. Shifting slightly in my seat, I watched the reflection of the thin looking gentleman. He leaned in against the pull of the train which was herding him counter to his inclination, all the better to see the inner mound of my right breast snugly nestled in that synthetic lace cup. I maintained this position until I caught his eyes reflected in the window. Then I opened my mouth slightly and leant away from him, revealing a little bit more. As the tube careened squealing into the station, halting like an overtired general at the end of a mountain march, I leapt out of my seat and enfolded myself in a mash of passengers spewing out of the sliding doors. I did not look back.

What was most wonderful about this phase – and it was a phase – was that previously travelling to and from work had been a chore. I had tried reading – newspapers, books – but the inconsistent ebb and sway of the train tended to make me queasy. Especially in the mornings, if I had not had time for breakfast. It was hard under these conditions to keep up with the plot. I persevered, but found that I would turn pages mechanically, with scant regard for the story, which seemed unfair to the author. After all, they had taken such thought in writing it. I was never one for music, and felt mildly jealous of those passengers who plugged earphones in for entertainment. Still, it was not really me. Yet, with several new bras in my collection, I was able to amuse myself on the train both before and after work throughout the spring months, and nearly into summer. I looked forward to the ride. Soon enough the weekends became a chance to explore previously unknown suburban lines. It was with the greatest diligence that I chose the most plain-looking and unassuming men to showcase a small sample of those beautiful and diverse fabrics, put well to their intended use, for I am a heavy-chested woman.

Wearing sexy undergarments is one thing, and has its place, as I had come to realise, on public transport. However, the hotter the weather became, the less clothing other women wore, and the tube became a general vista of overflowing bosoms trussed up in tight dresses. Indeed, the fashion was for plunging v-shaped necklines, which did not help my mission. It was harder to attract attention, given the competition on offer, as the communal gaze of the other passengers (male *and* female) fell on these wondrous and multiple breasts. Even I found myself looking down into the almost unavoidable crevice that formed between each pair on those unlucky days when I missed out on a seat and found myself standing in the carriage.

I would not have guessed it, and I'm sorry to say, but after a while the novelty began to wane. Those bras were never the same after I washed them, even though I made sure to use a gentle detergent and lathered them by hand. The act had started to become routine: find suitable man, pop open buttons, exhibit goods. For a while I simply experienced inertia, uncertain where to take this next. Frustratingly, the more I thought about it, the less I seemed to be able to move myself forward. So as a conciliation of sorts I bought boxes and boxes of frozen blackcurrant cheesecake, which I ate in large quantities without putting it on a plate.

That gluttony ended abruptly late one night when I caught Furry simultaneously eating from the same container as I watched Audrey Hepburn in 'Charade'. I do love Furry, and she is a neat little eater, but the idea of sharing from the same cheesecake is somewhat revolting.

Oval

With summer came the annual exodus to the cricket. Grown men pay good money to spend hours sitting outdoors in heavy temperatures, watching a few sticks stuck in a field, apparently enjoying themselves. The matches seem to play endlessly and seemingly in slow motion, broadcast on a large screen in the beer garden of the pub over the road from my flat. I can hear it. Inspired by Hepburn's little trench coat, with its knotted belt at the waist, I hatched a plan. The game needs livening up, in my opinion.

I didn't bother to call in sick that day. After all, I was certain that the reason for my absence would be known soon enough. No need to lie. I ambled down the road, past the post office. I bought a stamp and stuck it on the mangled brown package that had been idle in my handbag for the past few months. Knowing the name now, I wrote it on the envelope using the biro attached to a string at the counter, and posted it in the box on the street.

The stadium was full, and the sun was very hot. It was nearly the end, not that I really understand what that *is* exactly in cricket. I had spent quite a lot on my ticket, because it was the finale, if we can call it that.

I watched for the whole morning, just to get the feel of things.

After lunch and perhaps not surprisingly given the genteel pace of proceedings the crowd seemed quite sleepy. Getting up, I walked down to the front of the stalls. There was a low wall that separated the grass, slightly browning from lack of rain, from the tiered plastic seats. I didn't stop when I reached that wall, but stepped up onto it and jumped over. I started to walk faster now, briskly, and with purpose. I heard a shout, but ignored it, and started to jog. Breaking into a light run, I untied the bow at the waist of my wraparound Hepburn-style coat, casting it off my shoulders and letting it fall behind me like the flying cape of a superhero. I have never run naked, and certainly not in front of so many people. Yet I have to say that it really is the most joyous feeling to experience the warmth of the sun on your skin, *all* of your skin, and to allow your breasts to bounce freely. Due to my proportions, mine did generate quite a rhythm as I gambolled along. Bending forward to touch the wicket, I was accompanied by the crescendo of a rousing cheer. The click of a shutter and a flash went off behind me.

My glory was short lived, however, as two men came and held a hat and a bat respectively over my privates, though neither seemed to have anything to cover my backside. So it came to pass that I was taken for questioning by the police, and was eventually issued a warning for indecent exposure. In the languidness of the heat, with England a winner against Australia, no-one seemed to mind. The officers exchanged amused glances as I tiptoed away, fully clothed once again.

Envelope

Oversleeping the next day, I scurried into our office about ten minutes late, not wanting to talk to anyone. The daily newspaper was brazenly folded on top of your in-tray. I saw the black and white photograph. It was a striking shot. The players were captured static in time, standing in front of me, gaping mouths open. Play forgotten. The image caught my legs at their best, as I leaned towards the stumps: my raised heels contoured my calves and thighs into a shapely curve. I so rarely get to see myself from this particular angle and I liked the result.

The mailroom delivers the post in the afternoon, and as I sat, inputting data, I saw the familiar wrinkled envelope drop onto your in-tray, covering the newspaper. I stopped my work. You looked up, intrigued, as we don't usually get mail, and started to finger the package. You turned it over, and then ripped the top clean off, reaching your hand inside. You looked so innocent, so excited, almost like a child happening upon secret treasure in the garden. Your face lost its gauntness, and became placid. As you were lifting the grey bundle out of the envelope, a moment of realisation showed on your face, and you threw it away from you onto the floor in a desperate, ugly spasm.

You did most definitely blush, the second time you saw my bra, a violent, lurid red.

Contributors

Agnes Bairstow

Agnes grew up in the Blue Mountains. She has been writing since she was fifteen years old. Her work has also appeared in the 2010 Sydney University Student Anthology. She has a pen, a notebook, a laptop, and a beehive.

Hugo Branley

Hugo is studying Arts/Science. He seems to resemble the unfortunate madman in that anecdote who came down from the hills of Denmark to disintegrate the world with a syllogism. Therefore preferring Macbeth to the uncomfortably homely themes of Hamlet, Hugo spends his spare time in fabricating an infinite number of monkey-sized kilts.

Matthew Cai

Matthew studied Commerce/Arts and now works in advertising. He understands the potency of a 'big idea' and the way it can, executed correctly, transform X into Y. This is true for advertising, as it is for writing, and for art: the expression of ideas in creative and receptive forms. He is also really into film and acting.

Kevin Caucher

Kevin, originally named Chuyao Zhou, is a published short story writer, poet and designer. Beside his interests in art, he's also into observing people. 'Quarter after One' is based on his love for people observation, a bad break-up and a pop song.

Tasneem Choudhury

Tasneem enjoys everything from mathematics to poetry. He disliked high-school geography. He has a theory on time; you should ask him about it. No really, you should. You stumble along trying to find purpose in this world; he just stumbles. A life-long learner. An old soul with a young heart.

Martin Everett

Born in England, 1943 (he remembers the King). Left school, 1959. Halfway through his BA, majoring in Philosophy, as intended it is challenging the comfortably held views of a lifetime. He has never written anything before. The story came to him after a Philosophy of Psychiatry lecture on voice hearers.

Thomas Gardner

Thomas is an earthling and undergraduate. His interests include philosophy, poetry, classics, linguistics, and other such trumpery. He is delighted by the strange correspondence between language and reality, and the fact that everything means something, but nothing nothing. He would like some Demosthenian practice-pebbles and his own pig.

Christina Guo

Christina is an eighteen-year-old student who loves art, photography and writing. She is in unrequited love with inspiration and hopes that, one day, she will be paid to do things she'd be willing to do for free.

Petra Hanke

Petra is a 2012 MApplSc (Wildlife Health & Population Management) graduate, passionate for wildlife and nature. She got her first SLR camera when starting to work for a local newspaper during high school. Her first wildlife photography exhibition was held in 2011. Petra captured 'Melancholy' at Barossa Reservoir, SA.

Claire Hansen

Claire is a PhD candidate working on Shakespeare and complexity theory. Her thesis-avoidance methods include: tutoring, creative writing, addictions to HBO series, and planning trips.

Elizabeth J. Heller

Elizabeth received her B.A. from Cornell University and has a Ph.D. in Biochemistry and Molecular Pharmacology from Harvard University. She enjoys writing fiction and exploring Australia with her husband and two children.

Sarah Hilton

Sarah is an Arts/Languages student at the University of Sydney. She majors in Japanese.

Kelli Lonergan

Kelli is currently undertaking a Graduate Diploma in Creative Writing. She has previously been published in the *UTS Writers' Anthology*, the *AAWP Anthology of New Australian Writing*, *Seizure* and *dotdotdash*.

Celeste Moore

Celeste is an English major who divides her time between accidentally and intentionally getting lost in the city she now calls her home.

Joshua Mostafa

Joshua has studied in London and Sydney. He lives currently in the Blue Mountains, writing prose influenced by his various interests and obsessions: Neolithic Europe, proto-literate Sumeria, continental philosophy, bass-centric electronic music, archaic poetic forms, political theory, polytheism, comparative linguistics, and experimental narrative.

Elisabeth Murray

Elisabeth is an Arts student who is at her most interesting when she's sitting at her desk. She has been published in previous University of Sydney anthologies, *Voiceworks* and *dotdotdash*.

Kokkai Ng

Kokkai contributes travel photography to Getty Images and iStockphoto, partly because he was, till recently, a starving postgraduate with no disposable income. Awarded the Licentiateship of the Royal Photographic Society (LRPS) in 2011, he holds degrees in design and digital culture. He dreams of having disposable income one day.

Lidia Nikonova

Lidia is a Russian-born photographer currently studying Media and Film at the University of Sydney.

Drew Rooke

Drew is a third-year Arts (Media and Communications) student at the University of Sydney who has a strong passion for writing, photography and travelling.

Erin Martine Sessions

Erin is a 'pre-poet' who divides her working hours between figuring out how to finish her poems and being the 'too-loud-librarian'. In her spare time Erin enjoys adding to her collection of music and instruments, reading and writing poetry, and making trees out of old furniture.

Neil Varcoe

Neil has worked as journalist, barman, blood courier, truckstop attendant and as a lackey in a timber factory amid a freezing winter in country NSW. He intends to fall back on any of these careers if this writing thing fails to take off.

Rosemary Vickers

Rosemary grew up in a cold climate and disliked organised sport. When not drawing she read omnivorously. For many years she taught in Art Colleges, and didn't have time for serious reading. Now she has almost finished a Masters in English, studying for pleasure, and has rediscovered poetry.

Harriet Westcott

Harriet has a passion for writing and has penned fiction aimed at both adult and young readers.

Camellia C. Yildirim

Camellia once spent a lot of her time imagining what it may be like to be friends with Bret Easton Ellis. She is quick to judge people on their choice of footwear and books by their musty smell.

Wang Zi

Wang Zi is a reporter and page editor at *21st Century English Newspaper* under China Daily Group. He has been covering China's higher education for four years for the national news weekly, targeting college students and young professionals. He is keen on exploring how Chinese youth survive, adapt and change the transforming China.

Daniel Zwi

Jew. Happy to be published.

Editors

Maureen Chiu

Maureen is currently completing a Masters of Publishing, after having completed a combined undergraduate degree in Visual Communications and International Studies. With a background in publication design, she is an appreciator of fine paper stock and beautiful typesetting, and believes that you should judge a book by its cover.

Theodore Ell

Theodore writes, edits and translates, and his work has appeared in *The Italianist, Mosaici, Atelier, Modern Greek Studies* and *Earth Sciences History*. His own poetry has appeared in the earlier University of Sydney anthologies *Cellar Door* and *Sandstone,* and *The Sydney Morning Herald*. He is poetry editor of *Contrappasso Magazine*.

Pasquale Lazzaro

Pasquale is an English and Publishing graduate who would very much like to do this all the time. He harbours no ambitions, secret or otherwise, of being a writer.

Lauren Maule

Lauren is a fantasy geek whose greatest ambition is to find a way to live in a world with dragons, magic, liveships, immortal beings and twisted monarchies. Until then she has settled for reading about as many of those worlds as she can, as well as creating her own.

Vanessa Schlenert

Vanessa is a complete word nerd. She has surrounded herself with books her entire life, reading anything she can get her hands on, working in quirky book stores and writing whenever it takes her fancy. Editing comes naturally to this bibliophile, who has loved the opportunity to help shape these stories.

Anna Stelter

Working on *Sparks* has transformed Anna's passion for good writing into a passion for good editing. She hopes to pursue a career in editing where she can contribute to the works of great authors to come.

Camellia C. Yildirim

Camellia has a very large collection of the original *The Amazing Spider-Man* comics. She particularly likes the centre-fold advertisements for pet monkeys being sold for $3. She tries to convince the kids she tutors that comics and graphic novels are real works of literature too.

Acknowledgements

The editorial team thanks the Department of Media and Communications and the School of Letters, Art and Media at the University of Sydney for supporting this anthology annually since 2007. In particular we thank Dr Fiona Giles and Dr Fiona Martin for overseeing the project and co-ordinator Mark Rossiter for his advice, dedication and energy.

We thank Sydney University Press for producing the printed volume and particularly Agata Mrva-Montoya for her insights on technical matters and design.

Our thanks also go to Michael Vail and the University's Co-op Bookshop for their enthusiasm in launching this anthology and promoting it on the shelves.

We are extremely grateful to Mark Tredinnick for giving so generously of his time and for writing such a passionate and inspiring Foreword.

Finally, the editors would like to thank all the contributors for their creative efforts and for sharing their talents. We wish their future writing every success.